CODEX BENTHOS

CODEX BENTHOS

A CATALOG OF LOST MINES, BURIED TREASURES, UNSOLVED MYSTERIES, AND UNEXPLAINED ODDITIES OF VASHON AND MAURY ISLANDS, WASHINGTON

CECIL BENTHOS, PHD

Outskirts Press, Inc.
Denver, Colorado

Codex Benthos
A Catalog of Lost Mines, Buried Treasures, Unsolved Mysteries, and Unexplained Oddities of Vashon and Maury Islands, Washington

v2.0

Outskirts Press, Inc.
http://www.outskirtspress.com

ISBN: 978-1-4327-6299-5

PRINTED IN THE UNITED STATES OF AMERICA

First Official Edition

Published privately through the generosity of anonymous donors who do not wish their names to be known, but who wish to support the treasure hunting community on Vashon and Maury Islands. All inquiries should be directed to the offices of the author, Cecil Benthos, PhD, in Vienna, Krakow, or Bean Blossom, Indiana. If you wish to express sincere admiration, or have constructive suggestions, important clues, or leads to new treasures, you may email him at CecilBenthos@aol.com. Otherwise, consider taking a powder.

WARNING: Contains fiction. Processed on equipment shared with irony, pathos, satire, sarcasm, and unrestrained political commentary.

"This is not so much a book as it is an art project,
but then isn't life itself an art project?

The Author near the Lost Scotchman Mine.

About the Author

Cecil Benthos, a native of Munich, was educated in that city as well as the United States (at the world-famous Arizona School of Mines). He has advanced degrees in geology, mining, comparative religion, and extraterrestrial psychology.

Benthos is a distant relative of Erwin Rommel and a desert fox in his own right. An internationally known treasure hunter and entrepreneur, his profile in the treasure hunting community rose to prominence after he succeeded in finding the Lost Scotchman Mine in the Sonoran Desert.

The Lost Scotchman had long eluded others, partly because it was thought to be guarded by a legion of Apache Indians whose sole purpose was to prevent its discovery in an area that is held sacred by their tribe. But Benthos broke the treasure hunter's mold and enlisted a platoon of unemployed Civil War re-enactors who provided the necessary intimidation to allow Benthos unmolested access to the sacred site (no Apaches dared make an appearance), from which he then extracted the treasure, such as it was.

A subsequent charge by the Bureau of Indian Affairs could never be proven, and Benthos went on to search for another hidden treasure, the Mine with the Iron Door, outside Tucson. Here he met Fred DeGracia, renowned artist and collector of myths, who directed him to yet another fabulous cache, the legendary silver in the Llano de los Gigantes (the Plain of Giants), which supposedly was hidden by Coronado himself. Spending the next few years in Mexico was something he'd always wanted to do, and it seems to have been encouraged by the Bureau. It was in Mexico that he made the crucial contacts that allowed him to return to his homeland in Europe and establish offices in Vienna and Krakow.

Following the death of a favored uncle, Benthos inherited a property in Bean Blossom, Indiana, where he resides part-time for sentimental and tax reasons. His connection to Vashon Island came from his acquaintance with, and subsequent marriage to, world-famous Italian supermodel and blue film star Portia Sedan. They reside with their two gifted children and a German Shepherd named Nugget.

Table of Contents

Introduction (and Important Fine Print)

The people who live on Vashon and Maury Islands know very well how precious is their place in Puget Sound. Only about 11,000 people live in nearly 40 square miles, and they are surrounded by a moat that separates them from some of the woes of society.

But many of these people live in blissful ignorance of the numerous treasures and mysteries that surround them. This compilation attempts to remedy that, and to serve as a field guide for the novice Vashonite treasure hunter.

Our two islands have been known to Europeans for about three hundred years. Archaeological evidence suggests that a human presence was here since about 10,000 years ago, or roughly since one thousand years after the glacial ice melted and people could walk around barefoot again.

It wasn't until 1792 that Europeans with their written language, their big wooden boats, their smelted metals and their natty red uniforms showed up and explored the region. Capt. George Vancouver of the British Navy sailed into Puget Sound aboard the Discovery in search of the elusive Northwest Passage. Vancouver never found this, mainly because it didn't exist, but along the way he named Vashon Island after his friend Capt. (later Adm.) James Tiberius Vashon.

The first American expedition into Puget Sound took place in 1841 when Lt. (later Capt.) Charles Wilkes sailed into Puget Sound aboard the Porpoise (which was a boat), for the purpose of creating detailed charts of the region. Only generalized charts existed before that, presumably compiled by the Chinese in 1421. Amazingly, the Chinese saw no reason to return. Equally amazingly, Wilkes bore a remarkable likeness to Fred Gwynne (better known as Herman Munster) and would be played by him in the movie in years to come.

Wilkes identified Maury Island as a separate Island from Vashon (which has been a controversial call even to this day), and named it in honor of one of his expedition's surveyors, Lt. William L. Maury. Maury was portrayed in the movie by William Frawley, which one might say was a controversial curtain call.

Later, Russian and Japanese explorers traversed the area, both looking for pelts, precious metals, and other people (mostly women) who could speak Russian or Japanese. Although they did find pelts, some of which scurried away before they could "harvest" them, they did not find many precious metals, and all the people they met spoke what they thought was Chinese. I think it is mainly for that reason that they didn't get along with the natives.

Other explorers reached Vashon, too. Among them was a lost group of Polynesians (piloting a ship made from papyrus) who landed on Maury Island and tried to grow pineapple and breadfruit. Their colony did not survive long, but it is rumored to have been rich with treasures from the sea that were buried near the present-day Glacier NW quarry. This could be a unique archaeological site that should be preserved, rather than turned into aggregate or more airport runways.

As you might imagine, with all these people going and coming and coming and going, there were more than a few treasures lost and more than a few mysteries created. This book contains just a few.

With a little effort, and the clues in this book, you should be able to search for buried treasures near your home!

- **IMPORTANT FINE PRINT**: Lost mine and buried treasure stories everywhere have mythical components. Mind you, it only takes finding one treasure (as I have) to get one hooked. Also, be sure to follow the two basic rules of treasure hunting: 1) **Never trespass**; always ask permission to enter private property, and have a good idea of where you are (and where you want to go) at all times; and 2) **Respect and preserve the environment**; don't dig holes indiscriminately and don't muck around in streams, unless you can see the nuggets shining up at you; clean up after yourself, and leave only footprints. **Be careful out there**.

Lost Mines, Buried Treasures, Unsolved Mysteries, and Unexplained Oddities

The Baranov Diamonds

I begin my tour of Vashon mysteries with one that has been solved. Through the dogged and cunning efforts of two young islanders, the Baranov Diamonds were recovered in July of 2009. But before we reveal how that was done, let's review what was known of the diamonds before their discovery.

I first learned of the existence of the diamonds from my father. In the winter of 1942-43, while he was surviving the Battle of Stalingrad in an overlooked vodka cellar, he wrote several letters home that mentioned in passing some hidden jewels that he had heard about around that time, perhaps even as he was in the cellar. His letters were not clear, but as a child, I was interested in this. It was only later that I realized the importance of his words, and begin to piece together the history of the Legendary Lost Baranov Diamonds.

My father rarely discussed his wartime experience, and was not able to enjoy every holiday. Once, he confused Santa with an intruder and shot him in the nose with a rubber suction dart.

From what I could learn through extensive research in the Pacific Northwest and from my business associates in Russia, who almost refused being paid for their help, the Baranov Diamonds (my name for them) are a collection of brightly colored and rare heart-cut stones that came from a diamond mine in the Urals. They were originally a gift that Napoleon acquired for Josephine ("Stolen!" my Russian friends say), but were lost in the retreat of the French in the winter of 1812-13. Apparently, they were last seen then by a Russian woman who was paid to wash Napoleon's uniform, and she set them on his dressing table. They disappeared as if by magic that very day, leading some people to think they were indeed magic stones. Both magic and terrifying, is my conclusion, for mere mention of these stones has the power to turn some people into violent skeptics and has led to at least one traffic accident in southern Poland between a car and a manure spreader.

Not long after their disappearance, a similar collection of heart-cut stones was mentioned in a letter from Alexander Baranov, the first governor of Russian Alaska and manager of the Russian-American Fur Company, to his sister Irena. His translated letter contains the statement "*And dear sister, amazing stones are finally out* [or displaced] *painfully cut like little hearts my own like crystal* [part unreadable] *and colors remarked* [or remarkable]." So it was clear to me (as well as now proven) that Baranov acquired the diamonds and took them to Alaska.

Russian relations with natives along the coast during that time were strained at best, but following the Battle of Sitka, the Russians found themselves ill at ease in a country filled with violent and skeptical natives. Money and other things of value were sometimes kept hidden in case of attack. It is my belief, based upon the clues I have found, that either Baranov himself, or someone at his bidding, buried the diamonds on Vashon in 1815 or 1816 while returning from a trip into northern California. His diary from that time mentions an encounter with a native party that was prepared for war near what is now called Portage. The natives assaulted the Russians with beach rocks and sank a small boat. Oddly, Baranov wrote in his diary that he thought his men were being mistaken for someone else, based upon insults of a personal nature yelled by the natives, but this mystery (or magic!) was never explained. After the battle, Baranov was fearful of a second attack and so he buried the stones for safekeeping. Baranov never returned to recover them. He died in 1819.

Baranov's diary talks about burying the stones. Although the word "diamonds" is not used, he mentions hiding something of great value to be gathered when things settled down. He writes that the item was hidden within a tin coffee pot that was sealed with wax and mica (as was common for the time). Mica was also scattered near the hiding place, perhaps because it would remind Baranov of the sparkling diamonds, or perhaps only because they were careless with the precious mica (or ising glass). It was no coincidence to me that the words "ising" and "island" both start with "is."

And so, that is where things stood in early July, 2009, when I made available to the people of Vashon those clues in my possession and asked for their help in finding the treasure. The clues I had amassed included several rock carvings, some other artifacts, and most importantly a map. This map is partly a map that I found in the Hermitage in St. Petersburg, which cost me a fortune in pre-inflationary rubles (when money really meant something!) to borrow, and included some of my notes, as well as other notes I presume are Baranov's. The map in St. Petersburg had been cut into 12 pieces to ensure that no one had all of it at once, but two pieces were missing. Years later, I found the last two pieces in an Orthodox Monastery in Alaska, near Baranov's headquarters, stuffed inside a bible, one next to a passage in *Exodus* and the other in *Revelations*. The successful searcher had to locate as many of the map fragments as possible to find the hiding spot.

The treasure hunt drew about 50 searchers in a two-week-long search for the location of the buried coffee pot that contained 12 heart-cut crystal jewels. Two of Vashon's many talented youth found the treasure on the same day. Ella Maierhofer and Jesse Taitano, both 11 years old at the time, started the search separately on July 3. They each quickly assembled enough map fragments to provide encouragement and leads to where the treasure was located. On July 10, a critical clue was released at the Gusto Girls Restaurant, and that led to more hunting the following week. It was on July 14 that Ella first found the treasure. She and her mother located the burial spot, marked by a stone with a green spot and a scattering of mica, but did not immediately dig up the treasure. They were planning to return that evening. Knowing that Jesse was looking, too, they called his house and left a message asking if he'd like to come along and dig it up with them. That message prompted him to immediately jump back into the search without them knowing, and he also found the treasure later that same day. Fortunately for Ella, Jesse wasn't ready to quit.

Digging up the pot, Jesse removed the treasure and replaced it with a note for Ella to find later, which was the first of several clever clues that led her on another search for the final resting place of the jewels. Ella was led from one location to another around the island, each time finding another clue that directed her onward, until at last she found the jewels in a can under the north-end ferry dock.

Jesse and Ella with some of the clues.

Both Ella and Jesse worked out the location of the treasure with only 8 of 12 possible map pieces. Ella relied on her cunning and clever use of the internet and published maps, and Jesse relied on dogged field work reminiscent of Indiana Jones. For Ella, the best part of the search was the "Excitement and glory of the find. Unwinding the plot was a lot of fun, too." For Jesse, it was all about the excitement of finding the treasure.

And so it is with me.

Roxane's Golden Crown

Alexander the Great's legacy to human civilization and development in the Middle East and the Eastern Mediterranean region is widely known and revered. What is not widely known is that his presence is felt even on Vashon Island, where some of his treasure may reside today.

Until recently, James "Jimbo" Tarkanian was one of the hidden homeless on the island. A veteran of the war in Afghanistan, he went A.W.O.L. after his first tour in the northern part of the country, which in ancient times was called Bactria. Showing up on Vashon shortly thereafter, he would often be seen hanging out in town or strumming a borrowed guitar.

Jimbo had two "quirks" that proved memorable to those who met him: he always wore a backpack that contained something bulky, and he talked a lot about being on the run from the "protectors." Most people thought he was a bit daft when he started talking about the "protectors." Perhaps he was a victim of post-traumatic stress disorder or a casualty of too much drug use, they thought. Certainly, his failure to bathe added to that impression. But it was his fanatical devotion to whatever was in his backpack that caught most people by surprise. It wasn't long before people began to wonder just what was in that backpack and why it was so special.

After Jimbo's untimely disappearance, I assembled available clues and researched his history thoroughly. I interviewed his former Army buddies and contacted his family for more biographical information. I also gained access to the official military records through an old girlfriend of mine at the German War Ministry, who coincidently was at a loose end. She was able to access confidential records kept at the super-secret Department of Fatherland Security (so secret that I predict you have not heard of it until now) by employing a little-known Microsoft Word flaw (in the spellchecker) that to this day she refuses to share with me. She also helped me lower my mortgage payment that way, and she was always the snappy dresser, filling out sweaters to the point of distraction…but I digress.

It was those D.F.S. records that proved key to understanding both Jimbo's actions and his fears. Once I assembled all of this information, the answer became obvious: Jimbo had stumbled onto a fantastic treasure during his stay in Afghanistan, and that treasure's original owner was Alexander's beloved wife.

In 328 BC, Alexander began a campaign that would take him into present day Afghanistan, Tajikistan, Pakistan, and further into India. He battled kings and chieftains all along the way. While in Bactria (far northern Afghanistan), Alexander met and was married to the beautiful Roxane, daughter of a Bactrian nobleman. Some sources state that the marriage was arranged to cement his relations in the area so that he could turn his attentions toward the Indian subcontinent. But other reliable sources state that Alexander fell deeply in love with Roxane.

Little is known of Alexander's sexual history. Some say he was bisexual, others congratulate him on his self-discipline, and still others talk of him having many women during his expeditions. What is certain is that Alexander married twice during his lifetime, late in his brief life to Roxane for love, and earlier to

Stateira, a Persian princess and daughter of Darius III, out of political interest. According to some contemporary historians, his love for Roxane fully eclipsed all other relationships he had, which was just as well because Roxane later had Stateira killed. To paraphrase John Lennon, he loved them all but he loved Roxane more.

Weapons used to fight Alexander's army? Possibly so!

Alexander took Roxane with him on his foray into India. He crossed the Indus in 326 BC and won an epic battle against a local ruler named Porus, who ruled a region in the Punjab, in the Battle of Hydaspes. But Alexander also lost two treasures during the battle. First, his prized horse Bucephalus was wounded and died. Alexander had ridden Bucephalus into every one of his battles in Europe and Asia, so when the horse died Alexander was grief-stricken. He even founded a city in his horse's name. Alexander's second loss at Hydaspes was when Roxane miscarried and lost the first son she was bearing for him.

Alexander continued his campaign through the Indian subcontinent, winning glorious battles against all odds, constructing a navy of 1000 ships for travel to the ocean, and suffering a grievous wound when a spear pierced his breastplate. They reached the mouth of the Indus River in 325 BC and turned back toward Persia. His return to the west was just short of a disaster because of ill-timed desert crossings, mismanagement by his appointees, and misunderstandings by his troops that lead to mutinies.

Alexander and his army eventually reached Babylon, and it was there on either June 10 or 11, 323 BC, that Alexander died while staying in the palace of Nebuchadnezzar II, one month short of his 33rd birthday. The historian Plutarch gives a lengthy account of the circumstances of his death. He also describes the birth several months later of Alexander's second son by Roxane, Alexander Aegus of Macedon.

At the time of his death, Alexander's body was placed in a solid gold sarcophagus, which was in turn placed in a second gold casket. According to the historian Aelian, a seer foretold that the land where Alexander was to be laid to rest "would be happy and unvanquishable forever." It is perhaps more likely that rulers saw the possession of his body as a symbol of legitimacy. For this reason, Ptolemy of Egypt stole the casket and took it to Memphis on the Nile. His successor transferred the sarcophagus to Alexandria, where it was visited by Pompey, Julius Caesar and Augustus during separate pilgrimages.

In what must be the first record of a major faux pas by a prominent politician, Augustus (that same *Caesar Augustus* who ruled Rome during the birth of Jesus Christ) reportedly knocked the mummified nose off of Alexander's face by accident. This event led to the establishment of a number of early Latin clichés, such as "as plain as the nose on his face," but even with intense public scrutiny from the opposition party and threat of a filibuster, the nose disappeared mysteriously along with the reporter who had broken the story.

Alexander's tomb was closed to the public "for cleaning" in 200 AD and the ultimate fate of the nose-less body and its valuable containers remains unknown. An interesting coincidence between that time and the present day is that several American Presidents can claim to be descendents of Caesar "Nose Buster" Augustus, including Gerald Ford, who was known for his perfect golf swing.

There was a flurry of interest in Alexander a couple of years ago when the so-called "Alexander Sarcophagus" was discovered near Sidon. However, it turned out that this is not Alexander's sarcophagus, but rather it is someone else's and was given that name because it was decorated with bas-reliefs depicting Alexander and his companions. The real sarcophagus is still missing.

But what appears to be missing no longer is the small wooden chest that contains Roxane's golden crown. When Roxane was married to Alexander, she was elevated to the equivalent of Empress and was given a crown of laurel leaves made of gold. Being a humble woman, she did not want to take advantage of her relationship with the great Alexander. She refused to wear the crown except for special occasions, such as some birthdays and the occasional ex-pat Grecian orgy. The crown resided in a patterned wood box, which also housed a few souvenirs of her travels as she crossed India and made her way to Babylon.

When Alexander died, Roxane moved in with her mother-in-law in Macedonia. It was there in 316 BC that both she and her son were murdered by Alexander's successor. Historians note that they were likely buried at Aigai, the palace of Alexander's father, Phillip II, but history has lost track of her chest with its crown and assorted trinkets. One contemporary account describes the return of Roxane's entourage and belongings to Bactria following her death, but that account cannot be verified.

It is my theory, based on confidential information I received from Jimbo Tarkanian's family, that the chest and its contents eventually were returned to Afghanistan, and that the items were cared for and protected by a loyal cult of Alexander's followers, active even today. And this is where our intrepid American soldier enters the story.

Jimbo wrote an email to his mother just after his first battle that describes how he stumbled into a cave during the battle and found a unique wooden box filled with golden leaves. He stuffed it into his backpack and went back to his patrol, but was convinced that someone sinister was following him.

His Army mates began to notice a change in Jimbo. No longer the gay blade and trigger-happy warrior, he became withdrawn and distrustful. Eventually he disappeared and was reported to be absent without leave. Some thought he was captured and killed by the insurgents, but instead he turned up on Vashon as a member of the homeless community still wearing his fatigues and carrying his precious backpack.

The last time Jimbo was seen was on the most recent anniversary of September 11th. He appeared agitated and stated to some of his friends that the "protectors" were about to find him and that he had to hide his "chest." Four days later on September 15, his empty blood-stained backpack was found behind the Island Market with a cryptic note inside that read "*It is now hidden where no BODY, and no dogs, will find it.*" Along with the note were some

Russian cigarettes, a hunter's knife, a cat's eye marble, an Army-issue compass, and a copy of the James Bond spy novel *Goldfinger* with one particular female character's name underlined. There was also a list of numbers arranged in a square of columns.

I have that list. Across the top it reads "Left is 0." The numbers begin: 0-0-0-1-0, but there are too many numbers to list here.

Never attempt to cross a stream with a Volkswagen Beetle, despite what the car rental agency says about them being good field vehicles. Here I am stranded in the Black Hills of South Dakota with Chuck Lane and Dr. Paul Dean Proctor, both of whom were treasure hunters par excellence.

The Lost Lake Spook Light

For those of you who are uninitiated (which included me until just a few months ago), Lost Lake is a moss-filled wetland on the east side of Vashon Island near the south end. It's in the middle of a tract owned and administered by the Land Trust, so it's open to the public, but there is no legal public access to the site and no formally maintained trail to the lake. Still, those "in the know" park their car in a certain spot and walk an informal trail to this mystical and mysterious spot when they want to relish the flora and fauna. But the access is on private land, so I do not recommend that you go there unless you ask the neighbors for permission first.

Geologists call this lake a "sag pond." It's a depression created by landsliding where the ground is broken and rotated. The landslide of which Lost Lake is part is thousands of years old, but I suspect that it's still in motion. I suspect this because of the numerous odd occurrences reported from the lake, not the least of which is Van Olinda's story of the evil lake spirit as documented in his *History of Vashon-Maury Island,* first printed in 1935 and reprinted in 1985 by Roland Carey (Alderbrook Publishing Co., Seattle).

Van Olinda referred to Lost Lake as "Spirit Lake." The legend he relates has to do with a fearless brave who, while attempting to win a beautiful maiden, encountered the "Spirit (or Devil) of the Lake." The Spirit wanted the maiden, too, and so the brave and the Spirit went "mano a mano." In one version, the brave got the worst of it and his canoe was found upside-down in the water. In another version, the brave survived to tell the tale to his grandchildren. In both versions, the Spirit perished after being trapped in an underwater cave that connects Lost Lake to Puget Sound. Personally, I think the brave survived, and I think the Spirit is still there at Lost Lake.

Portion of a sag pond in the dry season.

The Spirit of the Lake legend is important because one version describes the Spirit as being a ghostly light the color of tree frogs. The legend relates that the Spirit floats through the forest as if attached to a cloud, keeping a certain distance from people, but appearing to want to stay near them as well.

The Lost Lake Spook Light has been known to European settlers since the late 1800s. First seen in about 1887 by Lars Olafson, a timber hauler who worked out of Tacoma, the Spook Light has been seen and reported by numerous fishermen, hikers, lumberjacks, and even an entire troop of Boy Scouts when temporarily separated from their Scout Leader.

A shrine reported near Lost Lake. Coincidence? I don't think so!!

Perhaps the best description of the Spook Light comes from an article that appeared in the local paper. In 1953, two teenagers went missing one night, prompting a massive search by their parents and the King County Sheriff. They were found cowering next to a large log, soaked with sweat, missing some of their clothes and badly frightened. The story they gave was printed in the paper, from which I quote here directly:

'Hank Whitmore and Betsy Miller, both students at Vashon High School, were found early Sunday morning after an all-night search by a group of volunteers. Both were in good shape, but cold and shaken by their experience.

According to witnesses, Whitmore and Miller were last seen leaving for home after the Harvest Dance on Saturday evening. Whitmore was driving his father's Studebaker. Hours later, their parents independently reported their children as missing and the search was on. At about 3 AM, Deputy Tom Walker located the Studebaker on a side road between the school and the Miller house. It was stuck in a ditch and one headlight was broken. It was from there that searchers combed the woods, eventually finding the lost teens cowering near Lost Lake. Their explanation created a stir among the searchers.

Whitmore stated that he turned off the main highway when a rock was kicked up by a truck in front of the car and broke one of the headlights. He stopped to examine the damage and got out of the car. It was then that both teens noticed a strange light further down the side road that seemed to hover just above the road surface. It was pale green in color. Whitmore got back into the car and put it in reverse, but the car lurched forward as if pulled by a hidden force and dropped into the ditch. The kids got out and started to walk to the highway, but were disoriented by the experience and apparently walked instead in the direction of Lost Lake. It was there that they again saw the mysterious hovering light, which was ghostly in appearance. They ran from it, losing some of their garments in the process, but the light seemed to follow them, always staying a certain distance away. Eventually, they found shelter on a bed of dry fir needles next to a large log, and the mystery light did not appear again. They were roused by shouting from the searchers, and were located at about 5 AM."

The two teens' experience is not unique. Many other people have seen the Lost Lake Spook Light, so many in fact that late-night hikes to the lake are now quite common in the summer, particularly among the teenage set.

No one has yet explained the mystery, but it is very interesting to me that some of the Indian legends describe the "Spirit" using terms nearly identical to the teenagers' descriptions recorded years later. This suggests that the Lost Lake Spirit is indeed just that, a spirit or ghost that pre-dates European settlement. It could be the ghost of a jilted Indian lover, which in the legend became the Spirit of the Lake. Or it could be the ghost of a young Indian maiden, perhaps caught in an eternal triangle between two suitors.

We probably will never know why the Spirit is there, but we can see the Spook Light anytime we want. If you are brave enough to hike to the lake in the middle of the night, give me a call, and I will go with you.

Blackberry Circles

Crop circles are well known throughout northern Europe and the British Isles, as well as in several states of the Union. However, Vashon and Maury Islands appear to be unique in that strange and mysterious *blackberry circles* are known to exist here but nowhere else.

Crop circles have been verified as proof of the activities of extraterrestrials, either as evidence of the landing of their ships or as signals left for others of their kind. Some are occasionally found to be the product of too much carbonated malt beverage and a vivid imagination, but few of them are just circles. Typically, the patterns incorporate other design elements reminiscent of atomic structures and the double helix of a DNA molecule.

Blackberry circles, on the other hand, are just circles with no other design elements. And although they have not yet been firmly associated with UFO sightings or other evidence of extraterrestrials, most are concentrated in the general region of the Maury Island sighting described elsewhere in this volume.

The blackberries that are affected are ONLY of the non-native Himalayan variety that is such a common pest and nuisance. This is an odd coincidence, that aliens may somehow control non-native invasive blackberries, but have no control over native species.

The typical structure of a blackberry circle is as follows: Within an existing blackberry thicket, the Himalayan canes begin to grow in a large circle, usually about 22 feet in diameter (seven times the value of pi). With continued growth, this results in the creation of a doughnut (or torus) of blackberry canes, inside of which there are no blackberry plants. Often, the center is devoid of most plants, as if it was a haven surrounded by a thorny wall.

These circles are thought to form in existing thickets rather than "de novo." As such, most are hidden and few are found unless someone clearing the land cuts through one serendipitously and notices its presence. As you might guess, this doesn't happen very often. But they can easily be seen from above, such as from a spacecraft.

Investigators have suggested that it takes about two years of growth to produce a blackberry circle, which clearly suggests that extraterrestrials are here on an ongoing basis. The numerous UFO sightings reported from Vashon (nearly one every night) would seem to verify this conclusion.

A good way to scout for blackberry circles, if you can pilot one like I can.

Anecdotal evidence has suggested that the blackberry circles harbor some type of alien healing power. Rabbit nests within the circles contain larger families, and animals that spend a lot of time within the circles live longer than others of the same species. Sperm counts are also higher in these animals. This fact has led at least one well-known island personality (whose privacy shall be respected) to sleep every night in the center of a circle that is near Pt. Robinson Road. Since he has been doing this, he has not gone to the dentist once, and his old automobile has not been serviced. However, he has reportedly started listening to Fox News and writing articles about property rights.

The life span of a blackberry circle seems to be about five years, which has been shown by one investigator to be related to Avogadro's Number, the number of atoms in one gram-atom. Clearly then, the biological impacts of being within a blackberry circle, beneficial as far as we know, are understandable.

What is not well known are the psychological impacts of these structures on humans or animals within or near the circles. Until that topic is fully investigated and the connection with Fox News discounted, I strongly recommend avoidance of these alien and possibly dangerous circles. Unless you count a future bounty of offspring (and college tuition bills), there would appear to be no treasure in them.

The Wife Smuggler's Cache

The story of the Wife Smuggler's Cache is a tale of deceit and treachery that is all too common in wartime, in this case during World War II. But it is also a tale of love and valiance, and it is those positive virtues that we must celebrate.

Ramon Dalisay was a Filipino farmer who had come to the United States to make his fortune and prepare a home for his bride-to-be, Ariyana Marikit. Ramon had promised Ariyana before he left home that he would arrange for her transit just as soon as he was settled in a place suitable to be called a home.

In love with Ramon for as long as she could remember, Ariyana was so beautiful that she was widely held to be the most attractive young woman in her town. Fond of wearing flowers in her long lustrous hair, she left a trail of broken hearts wherever she went, but only the faithful and strong Ramon was in her heart. Even so, other men pressed their case often, including a local small-time criminal named Nosantos Patacsil.

Patacsil was a "fixer," someone who arranged things in exchange for payment. Some might think of these payments as "bribes," but it was more just a manner of doing business at that time. Small payments were expected if you wanted to "grease the wheels." If you skimmed some profits along the way, or happened to mislay an envelope of cash, so much the better. And if you showed up looking for your payment with a long knife or a recently stolen Army-issue revolver, no one seemed to complain much.

Ramon arrived in the United States in late 1940, and he quickly found employment on one of the prosperous Japanese farms on Vashon Island. His employers found him to be both trustworthy and hard-working, and soon he was managing much of the operation. He loved this work, and also got to play baseball in his off hours, which was another of his passions.

On December 7, 1941, the Japanese attacked Pearl Harbor. Just ten hours later on December 8, the Japanese launched a surprise attack on the Philippines. An initial aerial bombardment was followed by landings both north and south of Manila, and the Americans were soon in retreat.

General Douglas MacArthur and his defending troops, both Filipino and American, retreated to the Bataan Peninsula and to the island of Corregidor at the entrance to Manila Bay. The city of Manila was occupied by the Japanese on January 2, 1942.

The brave defenders kept up their opposition on the Bataan Peninsula until April, and on Corregidor until May, but ultimately 80,000 prisoners were taken and forced to march to a prison camp 105 kilometers to the north. As many as 10,000 prisioners died from disease, malnutrition, and abuse by their captors before reaching the camp. Before the surrender, General MacArthur had been ordered to Australia where he escaped to fight another day.

After the invasion, the Japanese military organized a new government structure in the Philippines. Although they had promised independence for the islands immediately after occupation, the Japanese organized a Council of State through which they directed civil affairs. This lasted until October, 1943, when they declared the Philippines an independent republic. But even so, the Japanese continued to maintain armed forces in the country and directed affairs through a puppet government that proved increasingly unpopular. A growing underground resistance movement began to chip away at Japanese dominance, so much so that by the end of the war, Japan controlled only 12 of 48 provinces.

One can only imagine Ramon's fear and dread upon hearing of the Philippine invasion. The last letter he had gotten from Ariyana placed her in the gold mining district of Luzon, where she was working as a domestic. What he did not know until later was that European civilians and their servants from that district were rounded up by the Japanese on December 22, 1941, and interned at Camp John Hay, which was the U.S. Army's headquarters for that district. In April, 1942, they were moved to Camp Holmes at Baguio.

At Camp Holmes, Ariyana was finally able to get a letter out to Ramon telling him of her whereabouts and her health. She was fine, she told him, but others suffered more and they had little food and not much in the way of medicine.

Ariyana was held at Camp Holmes until late 1944. The Japanese administrators allowed postal correspondence with the outside world, but all of the letters, both coming and going, were censored. And it was in mid-1944 that Ramon chanced upon a way to get Ariyana out of that prison and out of the country.

By this time, Nosantos Patacsil was well established as a Japanese collaborator. Relying upon his skills as a "fixer," he arranged for favors for certain Filipinos and also spied for the Japanese against the resistance. Ramon had guessed the truth about Patacsil by reading between the lines of Ariyana's letters, and he decided to see if Patacsil could arrange for her release. He proposed this to Ariyana. She was to get a note to Patacsil and tell him that Ramon had lots of American dollars with which to arrange her freedom.

Ramon did indeed have lots of dollars. He was entrusted with the safekeeping of the entire farm when his employers were shipped off to a camp in Utah, and he had just sold a season's worth of strawberries. Ariyana wrote that Patacsil wanted $7500, a fortune for them, and Ramon proceeded to arrange for that payment. He found a way to get the money to Ariyana in early October, 1944.

On October 20, General MacArthur returned and landed with his Allied forces on the Island of Leyte. Fighting was fierce, but the Allies pushed ahead and cleared more and more territory of the hated occupiers.

It was in January of 1945 that Ariyana got word to Ramon that she was both free and residing in American-held territory. She could get transport to Vashon if he would make good on his pledge to marry her. Of course, there was never any question about that, and Ariyana was reunited with Ramon in San Francisco on September 2, 1945. On that same day, the Japanese surrendered.

Ramon was both puzzled and delighted to find that not only did Ariyana get out of that prison camp, but she also brought with her the money that was intended to pay Patacsil to facilitate her escape. How she managed that, she never said, and Ramon knew better than to question her. What people do in wartime is not to be judged by peacetime standards.

The happy couple decided to put the money aside for the future. Not trusting the American banks, who they thought were implicated in starting the war in the first place, they found a good hiding place near their rented farmhouse on the Westside Highway.

It must be within that hiding place that the money resides today, for they both were tragically killed about six months later just before they were to be married. According to one witness, a runaway tractor lurched in front of their pickup truck as they were returning from the market in town. Both died at the scene of the accident, their arms wrapped about each other in one final embrace.

Their possessions were few, but among them was a shoebox containing mementos from the war years. In the box is a note written in Tagalog that appears to be some kind of instructions, several letters, and two pressed flowers. As I am writing this, I can see that box on my bookshelf. Maybe one of these days I will find someone who can speak Tagalog.

Searching for the Wife Smuggler's Cache on scooter.

The Maury UFO Mechanism

Even a part-time resident of Vashon or Maury Island would have to have been in a life-long coma in order to convince anyone they had never heard of the Maury UFO sighting. Small children in the area can recite all of the details about the sighting. However, given that a few readers of this compendium may be unaware of the facts about this case, let me open this story with an account of what is known.

On the afternoon of June 21, 1947, Harold Dahl was piloting a boat and salvaging logs just south of Maury Island with his son, Charles, two crewmen, and his dog. It was there that Dahl and the others spotted six doughnut-shaped disks hovering overhead. Dahl later reported that the objects were about 100 feet in diameter and had a bright metallic appearance. One was wobbling and appeared to be in trouble. It dropped to about 500 feet above the water and was accompanied by the other disks that appeared to be providing some kind of assistance. After some sort of explosion, the foundering disk ejected hot debris that resembled cooled lava, with a shiny aluminum appearance, that fell in large flakes. The debris injured Dahl's son and killed the dog. Afterward, the disks rose rapidly and flew off.

Dahl and his crew headed to Maury Island where they stopped to assess the damage and take photos. Gathering up some of the debris, Dahl collected it and proceeded to Tacoma, where Charles was taken to a hospital for first aid. The dog was buried at sea on the return trip.

Dr. Benthos' charming associate knows so well where you can still find some of the UFO "slag" that she can point to the location with her eyes closed.

Dahl reported the incident to Fred Crisman, who was the harbor patrol supervisor, but Crisman did not believe him. Nevertheless, Crisman went to the location that Dahl described and recovered more of the debris from the shoreline, which he described as being there in large quantities. While picking up some of the debris, Crisman spotted another disk that he said dropped more.

The next morning, a man arrived at the Dahl home and invited him to breakfast at a nearby diner. Dahl described the man as tall, imposing, and wearing a black suit. He drove a 1947 Buick, and Dahl assumed he was a military or government official. Over breakfast, the man in black revealed that he knew details about the sighting that had not been publicly available, and he also gave Dahl a warning. Dahl was told he was not supposed to see what he had seen and that he should not discuss it with anyone.

Three days later, on June 24, a former military aviator and federal marshal named Kenneth Arnold saw nine similar disks flying across the face of Mt. Rainier. This sighting led to the coining of the term "flying saucer" and was widely reported in the press, both in the United States and around the world. Arnold was interviewed by local and national journalists, including Edward R. Murrow, and his account made headlines around the world. He was also interviewed by 1st Lt. Frank Brown and Capt. William Davidson, both from Hamilton Field in California. Oddly, 16 other sightings were reported of similar objects that same day at other sites in Washington, Oregon, and Idaho. Three of the sightings were in Seattle. Ten of them were in Washington State. The June 24th sighting by Arnold is commonly considered the "first" UFO sighting, but the Maury incident predates it by three days.

United Airlines Capt. E. J. Smith was a friend of Kenneth Arnold, but was skeptical of Arnold's story until July 4 of that year. On a flight from Boise to Tacoma, Smith noticed a formation of saucer-shaped objects near his aircraft. They first appeared just after nine in the evening, and re-appeared several more times over the next 45 minutes. Capt. Smith, Co-Pilot Ralph Stevens and Stewardess Marty Morrow all reported they saw the objects.

Ray Palmer, the editor of *Amazing Stories*, contacted Arnold and asked him to investigate the Maury Island story. Arnold agreed, and contacted his friend Capt. Smith for help. Arnold, Smith, and the two military officers who had interviewed Arnold, Capt. Davidson and 1st Lt. Brown, met Harold Dahl at the Winthrop Hotel on July 31.

Local artist's rendering of a crashed UFO, said to be an exact replica of yet another crashed UFO found on Vashon, but no information is available to the public on that particular crash.

Arnold, in his book "*The Coming of the Saucers*," states that it was about midnight when the interview ended. Davidson and Brown called for a command car to pick them up, as they seemed to be in a hurry to return to Hamilton Field. It was Air Force Day, the inauguration day of the separation of the Air Force from the Army, and all planes were needed. Just as the command car pulled up in front of the hotel, Fred Crisman arrived and took a large cornflakes box out of his trunk, presenting it to the officers. Arnold states that the material inside the box looked a lot like the samples they had in their room, which was presumably "slag" from the beach.

That was the last time Arnold and Smith were to see the officers. The next morning, Arnold received a call from Crisman informing him that the radio was reporting news of a B-25 bomber that had exploded and crashed twenty minutes after takeoff from McChord Field. The bomber had crashed near Kelso, Washington, and was the same plane that was on its way to California with Davidson, Brown, and the box of extraterrestrial debris. There were survivors, but Davidson and Brown were not among them.

There were also rumors at the time that the aircraft was under guard every minute it was at McChord Field, which was thought to be unusual, and there were rumors the plane was sabotaged or shot down. *The Tacoma Times* printed a story about the crash, stating that sabotage was hinted and that the plane may have held secrets to the flying disk mystery. Written by Paul Lance, the article stated the plane had been sabotaged to prevent shipment of "flying disk fragments" to California for analysis. The fragments were said to have come from one of the mysterious objects that appeared near Maury Island.

Reporter Paul Lance died two weeks later of unknown causes. The cause of his death could not be established, but Arnold later learned that the cause of the plane crash was a failure in the left engine.

An interesting coincidence in this case is that the Washington sightings occurred at almost the same time debris was first discovered in Roswell, New Mexico. The Roswell incident was first reported on July 8, but the crash site was discovered a few weeks before that.

There have been attempts to recover some of the "slag" from the airplane crash site, which is in a ravine near Goble Creek east of Kelso. The crash site is not open to the public, but resident Jim Greer did find some unusual rocks there during a recent search and presented one to the Museum of Mysteries in Seattle. In an April 26, 2007 article in the *Seattle Post-Intelligencer*, reporter Casey McNerthney describes attempts by researchers associated with the Museum to identify the nature of the rock found at the crash site, but no definitive determination was possible. My comment on this article is that had they given the rock to an actual geologist for investigation, results might have been different. Until that happens, we will know nothing of any value about the strange rock.

What I have related above is the official history of the Maury UFO sighting. You can research this topic in any location and find the same account, which leaves you wondering what really happened. Was the whole thing a hoax? Did Dahl and the others let people think it was a hoax in order to protect themselves and their families from the first *Men In Black*? What were those rocks really? Is it possible to get that many daft people together in one spot even if they are mostly from Tacoma? Many more questions occur to me.

But there is another part to this story. Through my investigations, I have discovered that another witness collected a fragment of the alien debris, and that piece has been hidden (and hence unnoticed) all these years. That fragment was found by one of the two crewmen on Dahl's boat. I won't reveal his name here for obvious reasons, but I can relate his story as told to me by his daughter, whom I will refer to as "Miss XXX."

When I first contacted Miss XXX, she claimed to have no knowledge of the missing item collected by her father. As I pressed her for more information over the course of several weeks and a number of nightly visits, she finally revealed that indeed her father had found an actual fragment of the alien spacecraft. But unlike the other pieces, this fragment was something mechanical, comprised of machined metal and of a decidedly alien appearance. She only saw it once as a child, but she remembered it as some kind of instrument, like a piece of a ray gun or something else just as foreign. Her father showed it to her only to impress her with its importance, and to warn her to never touch it or tell others about it.

Miss XXX's father kept the UFO mechanism hidden in a place not too far from its discovery, well out of sight of local residents and far from curious children. He was convinced that the mechanism was still somehow connected to the spacecraft because he claimed that it sometimes glowed, the glow coming from deep inside the mechanism.

Her father died without telling Miss XXX exactly where he had hidden the UFO mechanism. But she did find a cigar box among his effects that appears to contain some clues. Miss XXX claimed that inside the box there are fragments of glass or slag, a notebook with some scribbled notes and crude maps, several letters from the Air Force and one from Dahl's business, and an irregular mass of metal that looks like an aluminum alloy that had been molten at one time.

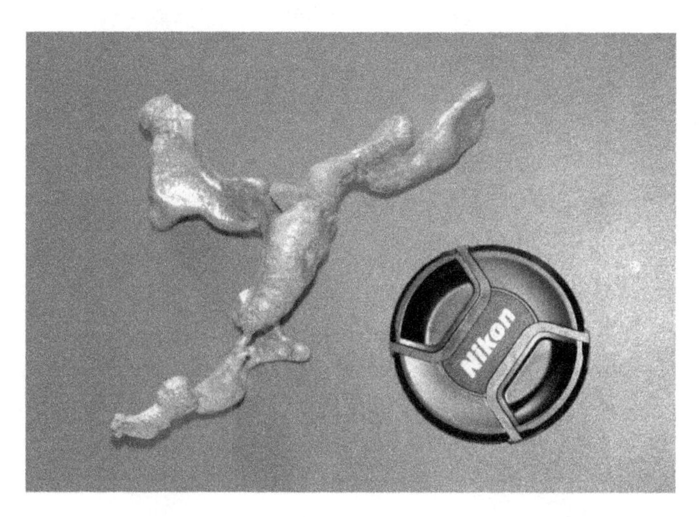

The molten metal fragment from Miss XXX. It is radioactive and stays a constant temperature of 67 degrees Fahrenheit.

As fate would have it, I had an opportunity to provide Miss XXX with some confidential assistance in correcting a tricky problem with her parole officer, after she was unfairly accused of a crime that has no victims. In appreciation, she gave me that piece of molten metal. It resides on my mantelpiece today. The cigar box containing the other items she has promised in the future, sooner if her parole officer makes more problems and we have to call my contact at the Department of Fatherland Security. Perhaps then, all will be revealed.

This YIELD sign, tastefully modeled by Nate W. of Ft. Collins, Colorado, was found miles from its original location, transported there by aliens.

THE MAURY UFO MECHANISM

The top of the Space Needle, rumored to be a spaceship posing as a restaurant (the excellent food notwithstanding), looks very much like the UFOs that have crashed on Vashon. Coincidence?

Two More Mysterious Sightings

There have been so many UFO sightings on Vashon and Maury Islands that I could not begin to even list them all, but there are two that are classic and about which I could not avoid writing. Both of these I discovered while I was doing background research for this compendium. One is described in a newspaper article from the July 3, 1893 *Tacoma News Ledger*. The other is included in a website compilation of water-related UFOs called *Water UFO – A Research Endeavor*, maintained by Carl Feindt of Claymont, Delaware. Carl has compiled 1165 cases that were reported between the years 1067 and 2009. The descriptions below come partly from those sources, and have not been altered or embellished in any way, much as I was tempted.

July being a month notorious for numerous UFO sightings, that month in the year of 1893 appears to have been no exception. The headline in the July 3, 1893 *Tacoma News Ledger* reads: *AN ELECTRIC MONSTER – Flashes of Light and Terrible Sounds Emitted by One in the Bay.* Clearly, something very unusual was seen that day, the likes of which only a few of us have seen here since.

Now, before you overload my e-mail in-box with vitriolic comments, let me admit that the events chronicled in the article in the *Tacoma News Ledger* actually didn't happen on Vashon or Maury Islands. In fact, we aren't sure where in the South Sound area they did occur, because the reported locations (Henderson

Island and Black Fish Bay) can't be found (at least by me) on any map. I found Henderson Inlet and Henderson Bay, both of which are south and west of Tacoma, but no Henderson Island. This seemingly minor discrepancy may cause some of you to suspect the credibility of this particular Tacoma rag, or perhaps to conclude that July 3rd was a slow news day. I prefer to believe that this newspaper article, like literally every other one of which I have had intimate knowledge, contains more than its share of errors. Once, for instance, I was referred to by the *New York Bugle-Tribune* (as reputable a paper as has ever existed) as "Professor Bendtoes." And claims by the *Cincinnati Inquirer* that I never finished my doctoral dissertation are practically laughable. I won't even begin to describe the problems they have at the *St. Louis Post-Times Star.*

Regardless of the potential for a few inconsequential errors in this published story, it is so bizarre and so important to the people that live on and near our islands, that I feel the article is worthy of being read in full. For that reason, I am going to quote most of it directly below:

> *A party of Tacoma gentleman have good reason to remember the morning of the 2nd of July as long as life remains in their bodies – and to quote the exact words of one of the party, "There are denizens of the ocean that man never, in his most horrible and fantastic nightmare, even saw the likes of.*
>
> *On Saturday morning a party, composed of the following well known gentlemen, set sail on the sloop "Marion" from the boat house at the end of the wharf for a three days' fishing and hunting excursion on the Sound. The party consisted of Auctioneer William Fitzhenry, H. L. Beal, W. L. McDonald, J. K. Bell, Henry Blackwood, and two*

eastern gentlemen who are visiting the coast, and it is from the lips of one of these gentlemen, who declines to allow his name to be used, as he says that shortly before he left the east he took the Keeley cure, and he fears that if his name was used in connection with this article his eastern friends might think he had "gone back" and got 'em again.

The party were well supplied with all the necessities of life, as well as an abundance of its luxuries, though it must not be inferred from this fact that the luxuries played any part in creating the sights seen on that memorable morning. Of course, as a person having much respect for truth, I merely chronicle the story as told me, and leave each reader of this remarkable yarn to judge for themselves the necessary amount of credence to give it.

"We left Tacoma," said the eastern man, "about 4:30 p. m., Saturday, July 1st, and as the wind was from the southeast we shaped our course for Point Defiance, intending to anchor off that point and try our luck with rod and line. We cast anchor about 6 o'clock, the wind having died out, and had fair success fishing. The wind coming up again pretty strong, Mr. McDonald suggested getting under way for Black Fish Bay, Henderson Island, as he knew of a fine trout stream running into the bay, and also an excellent camping place near the fishing ground. So about 8 o'clock we weighed anchor and shaped our course for Black Fish Bay, which place we reached about 9:30. We landed and made everything snug about the boat and made a nice camp on shore, and as it was by this time 11 o'clock we all turned in to get a little sleep as it was agreed upon that at the first streak of daylight we should all get up. About 100 yards from our camp was the camp of a surveying party, but as it was so late we decided that we would not disturb them but that we would call upon them the following morning, and would probably get some valuable pointers as to the best places to fish and hunt on the island. After a few jokes had been cracked the boys laid down and in

a short time everything about camp became as still as death. It was, I guess, about midnight before I fell asleep, but exactly how long I slept I cannot say, for when I woke it was with such startling suddenness that it never entered my mind to look at my watch, and when after a while I did look at my watch, as well as every watch belonging to the party, it was stopped.

"I am afraid, sir, that you will fail to comprehend how suddenly that camp was awoke.

"Since the creation of the world I doubt if sounds and sights more horrible were ever seen or heard by mortal man. I was in the midst of a pleasant dream, when in an instant a most horrible noise rang out in the clear morning air, and instantly the whole air was filled with a strong current of electricity that caused every nerve in the body to sting with pain, and a light as bright as that created by the concentration of many arc lights kept constantly flashing. At first I thought it was a thunderstorm, but as no rain accompanied it, and as both light and sound came from off the bay, I turned my head in that direction, and if it is possible for fright to turn one's hair white, then mine ought to be snow white, for right before my eyes was a most horrible looking monster. By this time every man in our camp, as well as the men from the camp of the surveyors, were gathered on the bank of the stream; and as soon as we could gather our wits together we began to question if what we were looking at was not the creation of the mind, but we were soon disburdened of this idea, for the monster slowly drew in toward the shore, and as it approached from its head poured out a stream of water that looked like blue fire. All the while the air seemed to be filled with electricity, and the sensation experienced was as if each man had on a suit of clothes formed of the fine points of needles. One of the men from the surveyor's camp incautiously took a few steps in the direction of the water, and as he did so the monster darted towards the shore and threw a stream of

water that reached the man, and he instantly fell to the ground and lay as though dead.

"Mr. McDonald attempted to reach the man's body to pull it back into a place of safety, but he was struck with some of the water that the monster was throwing, and fell senseless to the earth. By this time every man in both parties was panic-stricken, and we rushed to the woods for a place of safety, leaving the fallen men lying on the beach.

"As we reached the woods the 'demon of the deep' sent out flashes of light that illuminated the surrounding countryside for miles, and his roar – which sounded like the roar of thunder – became terrific. When we reached the woods we looked around and saw the monster making off in the direction of the Sound, and in an instant it disappeared beneath the waters of the bay, but for some time we were able to trace its course by a bright luminous light that was on the surface of the water. As the fish disappeared total darkness surrounded us, and it took us some time to find our way back to the beach where our comrades lay, and we were unable to tell the time, as the powerful electric force had stopped our watches. We eventually found McDonald and the other man, and were greatly relieved to find that they were alive, though unconscious. So we sat down to await the coming of daylight. It came, I should judge, in about half an hour, and by this time, by constant work on the two men, both were able to stand, and both agree that the moment the water the monster threw touched them, they became immediately unconscious."

On being asked to give some description of the fish, for it was, he said, "an electrical fish," the eastern man said "This monster fish, or whatever you may call it, was fully 150 feet long, and at its thickest part I should judge about 30 feet in circumference. Its shape was somewhat out of the ordinary in so far that the body was neither round nor flat but oval, and from what we could see the upper part of the body was covered with a very coarse hair. The head was shaped very much like the head of a walrus, though, of course, very much larger. Its eyes, of which it apparently had six, were as large around as a dinner plate, and were exceedingly dull, and it was about the only spot on the monster that at one time or another was not illuminated. At intervals of about every eight feet from its head to its tail a substance that had the appearance of a copper band encircled its body, and it was from these many bands that the powerful electric current appeared to come. The bands nearest the head seemed to have the strongest electric force, and it was from the first six bands that the most brilliant lights were emitted. Near the center of its head were two large horn-like substances, though they could not have been horns for it was through them that the electrically charged water was thrown.

"Its tail from what I could see of it was shaped like a propeller, and seemed to revolve, and it may be possible that the strange monster pushes himself through the water by means of this propeller like tail."

Dear reader, that was no fish. That was an alien spacecraft.

The second tale, as I mentioned, comes partly from the compilation created by Carl Feindt of Claymont, Delaware. His case file mentions that he took it from a book entitled "*UFOs: The Whole Story*" by Coral and Jim Lorenzen, published in 1969. I haven't read this book myself, but it may be worth investigating. In any case, the story below comes from those sources, and I am quoting in part from Carl's web site, which is an excellent and scholarly source for similar accounts.

The story goes something like this: On Sunday morning, February 18, 1968, three youngsters, all between eighteen and nineteen years of age, drove into a gravel pit approximately one mile east of the town of Vashon. I don't know of a quarry at Vashon Landing (about where one mile east is) and depending upon how you scale it off, one mile east may actually be in the water, so we have already identified a problem with the story, but let us continue, yes?

The youngsters drove their car through heavy rain to a point where the road ended at a pond. They then made a U turn at the edge of the pond, and the car was stopped facing north on the access road. After the car was stopped, all three boys observed a glowing object resting on a hill to the right of the car, or east.

The boys, Richard Frombach, Boone Powers, and Chris Beachner, described the thing as oval- or crescent-shaped and having a glow which they found difficult to describe. "A shiny type of glow" or "reflected light" or a "pale bluish-white" was the closest that the trio could come to a description. Thinking that they might not be considered credible, they drove into town to get additional witnesses. Frombach did not return with them, but they picked up Joseph Frabush and returned to the site. Powers parked his car on the main road, and the three walked into the pit area.

Upon rounding the curve of the road, they observed the object which had moved from its original position and was now on their left (presumably west). Frabush later said that he thought the object was lens-shaped, about the size of a compact station wagon, and made of shiny metal. He estimated the object to be about thirty feet in diameter. He also had difficulty describing the quality of the light but insisted that it was reflected rather than generated by the object itself, despite the fact that there was no light source nearby. This may say more about the nature of the object's surface than the light itself.

In Carl's account, Powers bolted immediately upon seeing the object the second time, and when Frabush and Beachner saw that he was gone, they ran for the car and they all drove back into Vashon to gather more witnesses.

By the time more people arrived at the gravel pit, the object was gone, but they discovered that the one-hundred-foot pond in the gravel pit had completely frozen over! The discovery was reported to Sheriff Don Holke at 2 A.M., and he went out to investigate. He was startled to find that the report was true, because temperatures in the area were then above freezing and had been even warmer for several days prior to the sighting. There should have been no ice on this pond! Investigation showed that small puddles bordering the pond that should have frozen first had no ice whatsoever, and the mud was not frozen either. Another unusual feature of the pond was the fact that the ice was very dry. According to all accounts, it was raining during the whole episode, making the presence of ice even more mysterious.

Other details uncovered during subsequent investigations included that the ice on the pond measured as much as three inches thick, and that it was formed in layers numbering from two to five, as if there had been up to five freezing cycles. The ice was also riddled with large numbers of bubbles containing air and dirt. It was concluded by investigators at the scene, who were presumably seasoned, that a hoax was unlikely because of the size of the affected area of the pond.

Carl states *"As far as is known, this is the first case in which freezing was a by-product of a UFO landing, and we can't begin to guess what the object was doing there or how it managed to freeze the pond if indeed it did."* Truer words were never written.

If I did not believe that UFOs could freeze water, I might wonder if the teenagers' sighting was alcohol-fueled. At least some of my own UFO sightings originated that way, or so I was told the next day, but I am not one to think poorly of my fellow man. I believe that whatever teenagers tell me, regardless of how wild, is the literal truth, and so should you.

Successful treasure hunters need to be prepared for any emergency. This one presented itself about a two-days drive from the nearest town in the Altiplano of Bolivia.

"Machine Gun" Morgan's Missing Loot

"Machine Gun" Morgan's real name was Jebediah Sterling Morgan. He was born in about 1900 in Albion, Michigan, and was drafted into the army for The Great War in 1918. He barely got through training and had just arrived in New York when the Armistice was declared. Although he never got to see France, he did get to see Coney Island.

Times were tough after the war, and Jeb Morgan found himself always looking for work, which was as scarce as duck's teeth. But with Prohibition and the easy money (and women) of the flapper era, Morgan found a niche for himself in Salina, Kansas, as a bootlegger. He wasn't a very good bootlegger, however, because his alcohol-making skills were not what they should have been.

After several explosions and an unfortunate episode with a valuable race horse that went blind, Morgan moved west to settle in Tacoma. His new girlfriend, Kathryn Thornburgh, decided that he needed a makeover, so she coined his nickname, "Machine Gun." He didn't actually own a machine gun, nor did he know how to use a firearm, but the name stuck. Small children and elderly ladies shivered in their boots when they heard his name, especially during the winter. Kathryn also began to call herself "Machete" Kate Thorn. No one understood why she named herself this, but some historians postulate that it may have been because she developed a "thing" about blackberries.

As times got tougher and his nickname-inspired ego grew, Morgan imagined that he could be a successful bank robber. He looked across the water and saw what he thought was a sleepy and helpless town with a bank: Vashon. Surely, he could knock one off over there. So "Machine Gun" caught a ferry on a Tuesday morning and walked into one of Vashon's early banks carrying an old carpetbag. This bank was housed in a building that is still standing. For reasons that will become obvious, I can't reveal just which building this was.

Morgan stuffed his hand in his pocket and pointed two fingers at the teller, Rose Dillard. Reportedly, he said "Do you know who I am?" Having just seen a Mae West film, Rose flippantly replied "Is that a gun in your pocket or are you glad to see me?" He told her it was indeed a gun. In fact, he said, "It's a machine gun." Not knowing that a machine gun would be too big to fit in his pocket, and thinking she might have just snagged a date for the evening, Rose emptied her drawers into his bag as the customers and other tellers watched in horror.

The bank president saw Rose's easy capitulation, and said to Morgan "If you don't harm anyone, I'll empty my drawers in my office, too." Morgan was thus enticed into the president's office and closed the door behind him. Only the two of them had gone inside.

Suspense hung about the bank lobby like a cheap suit. About 15 minutes later, Morgan emerged with what some witnesses thought was the carpetbag stuffed with even more money. He waved his two fingers at them menacingly and ran out. Instantly, the tellers checked on Mr. President (who was fine despite a severe finger whipping) and then alerted the constables. The chase was on.

Morgan headed straight south on the highway on a stolen bicycle, but as the sheriff was gaining ground, Morgan abandoned the bicycle into a nearby tree and started running. He was caught just a bit farther south, in an area now called Morgan Hill.

And here is where the mystery begins: Morgan's carpetbag was mostly full of crumpled newspaper. Other than the newspaper, all that was found in the bag was an odd seashell, a matchbook, a red lipstick, and a letter written by a female acquaintance of the bank president. There was NO money on him at all.

Running from the coppers is a crime, but not enough of one to convict Morgan of much, and so he spent only 30 days in the Vashon slammer (for failing to register his bicycle) and was released. He never returned to Vashon. It was reported in the *Tacoma Daily Gazette* that he died the following summer while visiting his girlfriend, having caught a bad case of the same thing that was killing the Chestnut trees.

Mr. President (whose name we won't mention because he still has relatives on the island) later moved to Port Angeles and tried his hand at raising chinchillas. He also died shortly after, leaving a pile of debt and no evidence of hidden wealth.

The amount of money that was "stolen" was never reported in the press, but it is my opinion that it was not a huge amount. Still, all of it went missing, and some people postulated at the time that the money never left Mr. President's office. How that could be is hard to say.

Are there any more clues, you ask? Yes. There are always more.

The Ivy-Replaced Man

On the hillside above Glen Acres Road, there is a small, well-hidden and crumbling marble monument (just a chiseled stone really) to one of the most mysterious occurrences on Vashon: the coincidental disappearance of a beloved islander and the appearance of his likeness formed entirely of English Ivy.

William "Bud" Tansy was a gardener's gardener. For years he ran a small nursery and catered to the gardening needs of his island neighbors, but his real claim to fame was his spectacular flower and vegetable garden. Stretching across two acres of hillside on the east side of Vashon, it contained the most amazing and exotic plants ever cultivated in the New World, including many species that were difficult to grow even in their home territories. Interspersed with these were native plants and trees that highlighted the beautiful vegetation of the Pacific Northwest. He loved his plants, and they loved him.

It goes without saying that his garden won awards; he was on the cover of *Gardening Today* a record 14 times, and was consulted by the Smithsonian when they had a problem at the National Conservatory.

For years, Bud was cherished by the gardening community, but there was at least one person who grew to hate him. At first, Bud noticed only that someone was stealing some of his small potted plants. He thought little of it at the time, reasoning that some gardeners had more ambition than money, and he could identify with that. When larger plants began to disappear, and even a prized vintage trowel, Bud alerted the sheriff. No one was ever caught, but the sheriff did discover a new trail through the woods marked by a trail of spilled potting soil.

The Vashon Garden Show that year was the most competitive ever. Several veteran gardeners were hoping to place against Bud's entry at least, but one, a man named Anthony Ragwort, was obsessive in his need to best Bud. A thoroughly distasteful man who was shunned by his neighbors, Ragwort was nevertheless a ruthlessly clever gardener who drove his plants into peak performances. He wore baseball shoes with spikes every day to aid his traction in the mud, and he often stomped plants with them if he thought the plants weren't listening to him or if they grew in a way he disliked. Unlike Bud, Ragwort did not respect his plants at all; rather, he cruelly used and abused them only to satisfy his evil desires.

When the garden show awards were announced and Bud had won again, Ragwort stomped out of the ceremony, poking holes in the floor, and was last heard swearing his revenge "*once and for all*." More than a few people were concerned for Bud's safety after that.

It was about 10 days later that Bud went missing. His friends and neighbors aided the sheriff in a search that lasted a week, but no trace of him could be found. Oddly, Ragwort also went missing about the same time. Neither of them was ever seen again.

Early the next spring, a lost hiker stumbled across what many concluded had to be evidence of the foul deed that ended Bud's life. Stretched out under a Douglas Fir was Bud's form, or at least a perfect replica of it, made entirely of intertwined Ivy vines. The Ivy had clearly grown that way of its own accord, careful even to reproduce the tiniest details of his face and hands, so that the likeness was indeed frightening. Vines had replaced exactly his veins and arteries. In the area where his heart would have been was the treasured vintage trowel, still slightly stained with what appeared to be blood.

The sheriff concluded that the trowel could actually have been the murder weapon, but with no body, he could not prove that there was a crime. He put out a warrant for the arrest of Anthony Ragwort, but Ragwort never turned up.

And that would have been the end of this story, except for one more unusual incident. A few years went by and the Ragwort property was sold for back taxes. The new owners started clearing out the overgrown vegetation that had ensnarled Ragwort's garden and greenhouse, and they found a large and deep compost pile. Lying upside-down on the compost pile were two baseball shoes and some tattered scraps of clothing. The compost had thoroughly digested Anthony Ragwort.

The Judd Creek Treasure

In Van Olinda's *History of Vashon-Maury Island*, there is a brief discussion of the treasure buried near the mouth of Judd Creek. According to that account:

> *Lars Hanson did a quite extensive logging business on the isthmus, where Burton now flourishes, and about the mouth of Judd Creek. He had married an Indian maiden, Katie, whose mother, Lemai, made her home with them.*
>
> *Lemai possessed a fortune of some eight hundred dollars, acquired by inheritance or sale of allotted land, which point seems to be not entirely clear, but nevertheless, a considerable fortune in those days, and of which she took very good care. It is known that she kept it hidden out--according to the best sleuthing minds of that day, somewhere above the mouth of Judd Creek. She was taken sick, lost consciousness and died suddenly, without any opportunity to disclose the location of her cache, and there it remains unto this day--perhaps.*

However, descendents of the early settlers who still live on Vashon have a slightly different story. According to one (whose name we won't mention, but his initials are S.R.), the treasure is $800 in silver coinage, and it wasn't buried on a hill or terrace above Judd Creek, but rather along the shoreline or even on the beach. Accord to another informant, it was buried under a stump. These people claim to have personal knowledge (through their ancestors) of both Lemai and her money. And they also claim it's still buried.

Native American settlements are known to have existed around the mouth of Judd Creek, as documented by archaeologists, so it would make sense that Lemai would make her home near that area. It is likely that she would hide the money a bit distant from the mouth of the creek, in an out-of-the-way spot. Or, she could have hidden the coins right under the noses of everyone who traveled that way. The obvious is often the most overlooked.

Clues to the location of the cache do, in fact, exist. I have in my possession a letter from Lemai that talks about her money, stating that she intended to leave it to her daughter, Katie, upon her death. She mentions in that letter that given her advanced age she will need Katie's help to retrieve it soon, and that they will need a good shovel, a ladder, and one other tool.

The need for the third tool is a complete mystery to me, and I've been in this business for years. Indeed, it is such a strange tool for recovering a treasure that I am reluctant to mention it here for fear of being thought a fool.

This letter is dated only about a week before her death, which suggests that they never had a chance to recover the money. Oddly, it is postmarked from Telluride, Colorado, a mining town famous for its unusual gold and silver ores, crusty miners, and fast women. How she mailed the letter in Colorado and got back to Vashon to die just a week later, is a great mystery. And why was she in Telluride in the first place?

Some of Lemai's personal effects are also still extant. I recently acquired several from an elderly gentleman who until recently lived in the Burton area. Peter Stefansdottir acquired these items years ago in an estate sale at a house near Judd Creek, and put them away never realizing until much later that they may hold the solution to this mystery. He sold them to me following some heated negotiations and a phone call to his ex-wife, who had considerable influence. His attorney was not so gracious in his reply, but ultimately I received the items in exchange for my promise to not make certain aspects of their history known, including that torrid affair with "Lucy," the exotic dancer from Tukwila about whom I cannot speak. Treasure hunting is sometimes a dirty and difficult profession.

There is also some question as to what Van Olinda means by "above" the mouth of Judd Creek. "Above" could mean topographically above, such as on the terrace where the highway bridge abutment exists, or above in a map sense, meaning to the north. It could also be interpreted as meaning upstream from the mouth. How these alternative meanings of "above" would apply to a hiding place on the beach is anyone's guess. And to complicate matters further, there have been three or four different Judd Creek bridges traversing the site, each accompanied by its own soil disturbance.

The location of this treasure would appear to hinge on both the meaning of "above" and the reason for the third tool, unless of course the personal effects offer yet more clues. But I leave that to others to solve.

The Westside Ghost Tractor

Many residents who live between Cove Road and Cedarhurst on the Westside Highway have seen the Ghost Tractor. It is commonly seen at about ten o'clock most evenings, and is usually described as a glowing pale orange tractor with one rider, always headed north from Cove Road. At times, the tractor is on the roadway itself, chugging along rather slowly. Drivers have reported coming up from behind it and being waved around, only to have the tractor disappear completely when they are pulling around to pass. Drivers headed south have reported passing the tractor as it's going the other direction. All of the observers report that the tractor is somewhat transparent and that it seems to shimmer as if the very substance of the visage could be disturbed by a gust of wind.

Sometimes the rider is a dark-haired man swinging a baseball bat. At other times, it's a beautiful woman with long hair who is wearing a wedding dress. Rarely, both figures are on the tractor, one driving and one holding on as if standing on the back axle.

The identity of the two riders has never been determined despite investigations over the years. Because the Ghost Tractor was first reported in 1946, some investigators have suggested the riders were killed in World War II. Others believe that one killed the other with a baseball bat and then committed suicide, probably with the same bat, leading them to suspect that one of the ghosts used to play professional baseball for the Seattle team. But so many sports personalities have been involved in such tragic incidents that narrowing it down to one pair appears to be impossible.

The strangest description of the tractor ghosts comes from an account in the *Seattle Times-Daily* from September 25, 1948. An article in that issue describes a harrowing event experienced by a young couple who had pulled off the road to "discuss church affairs" about ten o'clock a previous evening.

Peter Armstrong and Molly Manchester, who were "just talking," according to their statements, were surprised by both the bat-wielding man and the woman in the wedding dress, who materialized at the driver's-side window and proceeded to yell at them in a foreign language they did not understand. The female ghost was the most vocal, but the male ghost also made threatening gestures with the baseball bat. Armstrong and Manchester were so frightened that they immediately started the car and sped off down the road. Looking in the rearview mirror, Armstrong saw the tractor following closely behind until they turned the corner at Cedarhurst and left the Westside Highway.

Their story would not have been considered newsworthy had it not been for Armstrong's wife, JoAnn, who immediately filed divorce papers citing "irreconcilable differences about a so-called ghost story." Speaking later from his room at the Downtown YMCA, Armstrong confirmed to the *Times-Daily* that they really were just talking about church matters and that they really had seen a ghost, which was why he was delayed in returning home that evening. "The spirits were talking," Armstrong was reported to have said.

Upon reading this in the paper, his ex-wife was heard to say "Jim Beam and Hiram Walker talk to me, too, but I don't go out driving with the assistant pastor's wife when they speak."

A derelict cabin not far from the location of many ghost tractor sightings. Other ghostly apparitions have been reported here.

Giant Tree Frogs

The giant tree frogs of Vashon Island would never have been noticed had it not been for the disappearance of Madge Dunham's cat.

Madge lived fairly close to town in the direction of Fisher Pond. She was a valued member of the community and highly respected for her devotion to environmental and humanitarian issues on the island. Madge also was a long-time board member of the Community Council and chaired the Dispelled Rumors Committee, "setting the record straight for eight long years."

Madge's house was surrounded by large cedars and near a stream with adjoining wetlands. Her cat, Pickles, was a good hunter, and he often returned from his forays with a vole or a mouse in tow, to be presented to Madge as a gift. He was a proud and fierce cat.

Pickles' habit was to spend the afternoon in the woods and return about dinner time, when Madge would open a tin of "Tasty Salmon Parts" or "Zesty Innards Feast" or something similar. He would always come running when he heard the can being opened.

One evening during that season in the spring when the tree frogs are so noisy, Madge opened her can and no cat appeared. She waited for several hours, but still Pickles did not show. So Madge picked up her flashlight and started down the trail in the woods. She called his name, but still no cat. Finally, she was about to turn around and head back home when she spotted something shiny on the trail ahead. She approached it slowly and was horrified to find Pickles' collar and name tag lying on the ground, covered with drops of blood.

It was when Madge picked up the collar and turned to leave that she heard a loud and low frog bellow, coming from the bushes just off the trail. Instinctively she turned the flashlight in that direction and saw a pair of frog eyes staring back at her, but these eyes were the size of half dollars and nearly a foot apart. Startled, she dropped the flashlight and ran down the trail to the safety of her home.

The next day, Madge reported her missing cat and flashlight to the animal shelter, but the people who worked there were skeptical about her story of a giant cat-killing frog. After her story was reported in the alternative newspaper, she found that some of her friends were starting to avoid her. Children on the street snickered and pointed as Madge passed, and her cable company cancelled their service agreement unexpectedly. She even received an overdue book notice from the library. Oddly, the Community Council never said a word about it and continued to value her advice. Several Community Council members even suggested that she run for the post of President.

It was the overdue book notice that prompted Madge to research giant frogs further. It only took her a few hours in the library to find numerous references to giant frogs. She found that such creatures had been discovered in Guinea, Australia, Madagascar, and even southern France, where they were driven to extinction by local epicureans. A poisonous species was discovered in the heart of the Amazon Basin, and a toad-like variety was found at a secluded spring-fed lake in the Chihuahuan desert. All of them were carnivorous. One drug dealer's pit bull was found stripped of flesh near the spring-fed lake in Mexico. Clearly, these frogs were not to be taken lightly.

Madge also discovered that Native American myths and creation stories are peppered with references to giant carnivorous frogs, similar to their references to Crow and Coyote. So how was it that European Americans could have lived here so long and not noticed these evil creatures? Were the giant Vashon frogs Pleistocene throw-backs? Or were they descended from a pet that had outgrown its container, like the huge alligators in the New York sewers?

Madge didn't really care how the frog that killed her cat got here. What she cared about was Pickles, and getting revenge for his horrible death. And so she set out to plan her conquest or capture of the terrible beast. Madge told a few close friends about it, and although they thought she was clearly over the edge, they listened and offered to get her another kitten. But a kitten was not what she wanted, at least not unless she could use it as bait. Madge wanted frog blood.

I wish I could say that I knew how she planned to capture or kill the frog. All I have been able to discover is that Madge was last seen buying materials at the hardware store that could have been used to construct a giant gig. She had also purchased a truck-mounted spotlight and some hip waders. Beyond that, no one knows what happened to Madge Dunham. Her daughter found her cabin empty two months later, with about a month's worth of mail filling the mailbox and three deliveries of pears from *Harry and David's* sitting unopened on the porch.

CODEX BENTHOS

The only clues to Madge's disappearance were these cryptic notes, scribbled on the scrap of a torn Thriftway bag: "Frog can't see directly behind...use copper spear...don't forget ear protection...<u>never</u> move library."

The Aztec Figurine

One of Vashon's most colorful characters of the last century was "Texas Jack" Skippel. "TJ" as he was affectionately known (mostly by people who did not like Texans), lived on the island only a short time, from roughly 1936 to 1939.

TJ's real name was Jackson Robert Skippel and he hailed from Nashville, Tennessee. His childhood was burdened because he was given the nickname of J-Bob, which he thoroughly detested. In later years, that name would inspire the creation of a nationwide chain of steakhouses, but in the early 20th century, his nickname was not considered complimentary. Spending two summers with his aunt in Pampas, Texas, was enough to justify (in his mind anyway) calling himself "Texas Jack," which he did beginning in about 1918, just as the Great War ended.

TJ had spent the war years with a distant relative in Carlsbad, New Mexico, and had passed many days by wandering the hills and mountains in search of adventure and fortune. The borderlands were full of surprises, as well as bandits, in those days, and he learned to love life surrounded by rounders, cowboys, drunks, gamblers, and loose women. It wasn't long before TJ spoke fluent Spanish and found himself wandering the back roads of Mexico, even as far south as Mexico City.

It was in northern Mexico in 1916 that TJ ran into Pancho Villa's revolutionary group, and traveled with them for a while during the days when Villa's star was fading. Villa was on the run from General

Pershing and his soldiers from the 8th Army out of Ft. Bliss, having just made a cross-border attack on Columbus, New Mexico. Villa had raided Columbus because the U.S. government chose to recognize Villa's rival, the Carranza regime, and also because bullets that the U.S. had sold Villa proved defective, leading to the loss of some of his troops in battle. That is actually true. The United States remains to this day one of the largest weapon exporters on the planet. We are selling arms as I write this to the Iraqis and the Afghans. "*Your tax dollars at work*," says the sign on the highway.

Villa liked young TJ and introduced him to other colorful personalities south of the border. It was at this time that Villa was having trouble financing his campaign, having lost the contributions that earlier came from the U.S. The German government offered some support, but Villa was either unwilling or unable to benefit much from their entreaties. Even so, Villa and all of his associates were portrayed as German sympathizers, which served the propaganda ends of both Carranza and Woodrow Wilson.

TJ first met Pancho Villa near this site in northern Chihuahua, not far from Columbus, New Mexico (photograph courtesy The Department of Fatherland Security).

THE AZTEC FIGURINE

With support from competing governments waning, Villa turned to other sources of revenue, including the looting and sale of pre-Columbian artifacts. He was assisted in this effort by young TJ, who occasionally kept a piece or two for himself as payment. I hypothesize that this was how TJ acquired the Aztec figurine that resides to this day on Vashon.

TJ's whereabouts between 1920 and 1936 are largely unknown. He is said to have spent some time in California, hanging out with actors and actresses in the budding film industry. For the most part, they were rounders and drunks, too, so TJ may have felt quite at home there. He was even photographed once at Hearst Castle near San Simeon, but he is thought to have spent many of those years in Europe. In retrospect, that may have been an unfortunate choice.

Arriving on Vashon in 1936, TJ quickly made friends with the local rounders and drunks, of which there were more than a few. He was known for his quick wit, his knowledge of history, and his unusual interest in the airplane industry across the water in Seattle. TJ even tried to get a job with the Boeing Airplane Company, but rumors about his time spent in Europe and his past connections with the Germans kept him from obtaining a job. Considering that Boeing was soon to begin the production of bombers for the Allied forces, it was probably good that TJ did not find employment there.

His friends were also aware that TJ had a collection of Aztec artifacts, including one particularly unusual piece that was described as being "a little bit naughty." The naughty piece was thought to be the most valuable, and he kept it hidden separate from the rest, with the idea that it would help fund his retirement. The rest were expendable if TJ needed day-to-day expenses, but not the naughty one.

It was after the Germans invaded Poland in September of 1939 that things began to get hot for TJ. Accused by his drinking buddies of being aligned with the Third Reich, he soon was ostracized from most of the island watering holes and began to make plans to leave for parts unknown, but he never had time to plan an organized retreat.

Acting on a tip from a jilted lover, FBI agents raided TJ's house on Pt. Robinson Road looking for evidence linking him to the Germans. Failing to catch him at home, they found only a half-packed suitcase and his collection of artifacts ready to be shipped. The naughty one was missing from the collection, but there were some notes describing its location, in some form of code, as well as letters between him and a contact in Berlin discussing the collection in general and the naughty piece in particular. There was also a radio transmitter tuned to the frequency used by the Coast Guard lighthouse keepers throughout Puget Sound.

Texas Jack Skippel was never caught, nor was he seen again on Vashon Island. A few years ago, my associates in Krakow discovered manifests suggesting he traveled to Danzig (now Gdansk) and later to Vienna. We also found a letter to him from someone in Mexico City, but TJ's final resting place is unknown.

With the manifests, my associates found traced copies of the coded notes, which had apparently been mailed to Berlin before Skippel skipped town. Later, we also located several of the letters that were found in his abandoned house. They had been "saved" by one of the G-men who took them for his son, a stamp collector. One of the letters mentions that the naughty figurine "ought to be" hidden near the lighthouse. Perhaps the coded notes describe exactly where.

The coded notes of Texas Jack Skippel refer to some feature like this, pictured in a photo found during a house demolition near Racoma Beach. I have not yet been able to identify this feature, or its exact location.

The Lost Swede Placer

Few people think of Vashon or Maury Islands as centers for mining of gold, silver, or platinum. There are two known exceptions to that thinking: the massive amounts of gold known to exist on the Glacier NW property, and the even more massive amounts of all three metals waiting to be recovered from the seawater surrounding the island. As of this writing, it appears that Glacier NW may be prevented from mining the precious lode they own, the value of which far exceeds any amount of gravel, so I won't speak any further about that. I also won't speak about the seawater mining venture, except to say that the amount of precious metal dissolved in seawater is truly astronomical. Fortunately, I just tied up the entire project by investing all of my retirement funds and buying the last shares of stock. By this time next year I will be a very rich man!!

There is a third deposit of precious metal somewhere on the island. I refer, of course, to the Lost Swede Placer, which has been known to the old-timers (and briefly mentioned in the literature) since at least 1915.

Marten Petterson came to Vashon about 1900. He worked for years as a carpenter and woodcutter and lived in a sparse cabin near the town center. Too poor even to afford window glass, no one suspected that Marten knew anything about mining or gold, but he had come here from the gold fields of the Klondike, where he had learned how gold was trapped in streambeds and how it could be recovered. Only his closest friends knew that he had moved here from the gold fields unwillingly, until "things blew over in Skagway."

One of the reasons he was so poor was that he was also forgetful. He seemed to forget where he worked, or what time it was, or even occasionally where he lived. He forgot to tell the ladies about his estranged wife in Skagway, and when it was time for the bar tab to be paid, he forgot where he put his wallet. So it was no surprise to the people of Vashon to discover that Marten had forgotten just exactly where he had found his gold.

It was when he was on his deathbed and nearly delirious that his gold was discovered. Marten's friend, Tessie Skalgard, was straightening up his room when she found the tin can full of nuggets while examining his bed curtains. She mentioned it to her friends, and soon the whole town was aware that the Old Swede was sitting (or rather lying) on a fortune.

Several town folk came together that evening and coerced the old miner, who was drifting in and out of consciousness, to tell his story. The story was so fantastic that at first they did not believe it.

Marten told of his early days on Vashon when he was logging and looking for land for himself. He often wandered off into the woods and, being forgetful, easily got lost. It was on one of those trips that he stumbled into a gravel-lined creek bed and saw the sparkling yellow grains that were now under his bed. Using an old lunch pail to pan the gravel, Marten quickly recovered all he could find and stuffed it in his pockets. It amounted to about 14 pounds as near as he could figure, almost tearing his clothing from the weight.

Marten next marked the site with a blaze on a tree, in the shape of a chevron. He looked around for landmarks and noticed a rock pinnacle a slight bit to the northeast. Figuring that it was time to head home and register his claim to the mine, he started to look for a way back and realized that he was lost once again.

Thinking that he'd reach the Sound if he just kept walking downstream, Marten did just that and eventually came out on the beach, scratched and muddy, but he did not recognize the stretch of beach on which he had landed. Marten thought it was on the west side judging from the angle of the sun and the time of day, but it's so easy to get your directions confused at times like that. Instead of worrying about it just then, he hailed a passing boat and hitched a ride to the closest landing at which they had business. The boat finally landed at Ellisport after a very long ride around what Marten thought must have been half the island.

What was not clear from Marten's explanation was whether he was on the west side of Vashon Island or the west side of Maury Island. Given the amount of gold reported to exist on the Glacier property, it would make sense to look for more on Maury Island, but Marten also had worked on Vashon near Needle Creek.

Skeptics will take some comfort from the fact that no gold has been produced on Vashon, which would prompt them to doubt Marten's veracity. There are no known bedrock outcrops either, they might add, that could form a pinnacle. I'd like to answer that by saying that gold is commonly found in glacial drift in both continental and alpine settings. Glacially derived gold has been found in all states of the American Midwest, and was even found in a hole dug by the Cincinnati and Suburban Bell Telephone Company in far southern Ohio as late as 1965. I have the account of that discovery in their company newsletter to prove it.

Indeed, deposits of gold nuggets and dust in glacial gravels have been mined at Leadville, Aspen, and Silverton, Colorado, as well as along a number of other streams draining the Rocky Mountains. Glacial gold has also been mined at Virginia City, Montana, in central Oregon, and at several sites in British Columbia. If the rocks over which the glacier moved contained gold, then so did the gravels carried by the glacier. And that is how the shiny yellow metal, so treasured by man, was brought to Vashon and Maury Islands, carried along by the ice in sand and gravel. When the ice melted, the heavy gold concentrated in streambeds, where such deposits are called "placers."

Dredging and sluicing for gold on Maury Island.

When Marten Petterson died without any heirs, the town fathers decided to split the gold between the "interested parties" and a couple of public works projects (including a marble headstone for the father of the mayor's girlfriend). A number of people were thus blessed with newfound wealth, but only one saved part of her share for future generations, Marten's beloved friend, Tessie Skalgard.

Tessie kept the original tin can for years, along with one or two nuggets she hadn't sold, as well as a few other treasures from Marten's effects. She could be seen wandering the back roads and obscure valleys of the west sides of Vashon and Maury Islands, to "bird watch," she claimed, for a number of years. One night after too much tequila, Tessie mentioned to a friend that she had clues to the whereabouts of the lost placer deposit. She had found them in Marten's effects and kept them in the old can.

I have that old can here in my study. Besides one gold nugget, it contains what appears to be a rudimentary map, an old pocket knife with an ebony handle, four postcards from Marten's wife, one of which is addressed to Tessie, a can of snuff, and three old dimes. The message to Tessie is very interesting indeed.

All of that shiny stuff really is gold. Really.

The Case of the Reptilian Attorney

The cynics among you, dear readers, may contend that "reptilian attorney" is redundant, but I for one keep an open mind about such matters, because as a treasure hunter I am well aware of the strange and mysterious happenings in our universe. For instance, there are reptilian creatures that are not attorneys, and there are attorneys (mostly retired) who are no longer reptilian, as odd as that may seem.

For reasons that should be obvious to even the uninitiated, the particulars of this history have to be kept "under cover," but so compelling is this story, and so universal is its message, that I can't help but include it in this compendium.

It was about 20 years ago that our attorney first discovered he was changing. He had started his career by representing homeless and down-on-their-luck people in small claims court. But then he lost his altruistic bent entirely and turned to representing small-time crooks and drug pushers, including some who were caught near the middle school. A couple of years passed and our attorney graduated to representing white collar criminals, other attorneys who were accused of one thing or another, and public servants who had gone bad. Coincidently, it was about then that he started to get ideas about ways he could avoid laws, like those requiring you to pay income tax and get a driver's license.

It was shortly after our attorney completed his second book tour, promoting his two-volume diatribe entitled *"Get Off My*

Land: A Guide To Keeping The Government Out Of Your Business," that his wife noticed a green and scaly patch on his lower back. Slowly it spread to cover the rest of his back, and by the time he decided to pay a doctor to examine it (he had refused health insurance also), the "rash" had spread over most of his torso. This was the beginning of a total transformation that some of his close legal friends referred to as "his awakening." People outside the legal profession mistakenly thought his associates were referring to something else entirely.

The attorney's appearance became more and more lizard-like. His fingers and nails lengthened, his legs shortened, and he began to grow a tail. Oddly, his career was peaking at this time, and he had numerous high-profile corporate clients, the tobacco industry, and half of Wall Street on retainers. He was invited to speak to the American Bar Association so many times that some members (who also looked a little green) began to feel left out. "Give us a chance!" they'd say, while keeping a lookout for uninsured motorists, whiplash victims, and errant flies. But his wife was growing increasingly disturbed about this turn of events. It seems that she still had a sense of ethics and professional duty that caused her to be repelled by her husband's cold-blooded nature. A short time later, she packed her bags and left to go live with her sister in Florida.

It was all downhill from there for our hapless attorney. Following a brief encounter with an unnamed elected official, his transformation neared completion. Now too green and scaly to be comfortable in public, and finding that he was losing his voice, our attorney retreated to his house and basically just dropped out of sight.

Three months later, his wife returned to gather up some photographs and personal things. She found the house dark, with two windows broken and the front door slightly ajar. She slowly pushed it open and discovered an incredible mess inside. Papers and household goods were scattered all over the floor and a pungent smell was coming from the refrigerator, which had become unplugged.

While she was gingerly winding her way through the mess, a large green lizard jumped out of a pile of seat cushions and ran past her for the door. The lizard stopped, turned, and looked at her with a most pathetic expression. It let out a low raspy hiss and slithered away, never to be seen by her again. The attorney's wife grabbed a few things and left the island forever.

As the years went by, the house succumbed to the forces of nature and was judged a hazardous structure. The County Building Department removed the remains of the house and restored the building site. No trace can be seen of the house today.

But if you are ever tent camping on the south end of the island and you hear a low raspy hiss off in the brush in the middle of the night, you might want to zip up your flaps. The Legal Lizard, as he's known, reportedly gets very hungry.

The Postal Clerk's Retirement

This lost treasure is of a most unusual kind: one that is supposedly worth nearly a million dollars, but it may be so small that it can be easily hidden right under a person's nose.

Henry Butterworth (not his real name) was a postal clerk on Vashon, and he worked a number of years in both the Burton and the Vashon post offices. Henry was also a philatelist and a champion Ping Pong player, but he was not much for socializing. As a result of his eccentric habits and sometimes short temper, he was estranged from most of his family. Henry was, in fact, a loner. And not just a loner, but a conspiracy-theory looney who was thankful the Post Office introduced self-adhesive stamps because he was worried the Government could effect mind control by putting chemicals in the stamp glue.

Henry lived alone in a small apartment in the upstairs of a two-story house in Burton. He had a Ping Pong table in his living room, and late into the night the tenant below could hear him batting the Ping Pong ball around. Henry was such a loner, you see, that he had perfected the game of one-person Ping Pong. He played by himself for hours and hours.

He also spent many evenings alone in a restaurant/bar that was housed in the same location as a currently operating restaurant, whose name I cannot share in this book. In fact, much of the furniture (tables and bar stools) in use then are still being used today. If you've ever eaten at this restaurant, which you likely have, you may have parked your fanny on Henry's favorite stool.

Henry's second hobby, stamp collecting, was more in line with his day job. He didn't know much about stamps, but he really enjoyed collecting and arranging them in albums.

Henry would sometimes ask mail recipients at the Post Office if he could have the stamps that came on letters to them, particularly if they were from distant places that were warm and tropical. He actually got into a fight once in the Post Office lobby over a stamp that pictured a topless Polynesian woman in a grass skirt doing the Hula. That fight caused him to be disciplined by the Postmaster, and he temporarily lost his mail sorting job and was assigned to truck maintenance. Henry later told his aunt that those days were the worst of his entire life.

Henry also thought that he had found the perfect way to save for his retirement. Being disgruntled with the government retirement plan, he added to this savings by snagging every single piece of junk mail that contained a penny or a nickel or a dime. You know these pieces, from the *Return the Manatees to Puget Sound Repatriation Fund* or the *Starving Children in Hollywood Relief Fund*, each with a single coin attached as some sort of marketing ploy. Perhaps you can imagine how many such mailings go through a single post office: to be precise, LOTS. Henry grabbed them all and saved the coins, reasoning that not a single person would be concerned about receiving less junk mail. After a period of time, he had amassed a savings that approached the high six figures, all from nickels and dimes.

But Henry was not suspected of any serious wrongdoing until after several registered letters went missing. They all seemed to disappear when he was on duty. It was claimed that at least one contained a substantial amount of money. The others contained money orders, checks, and other negotiable securities. All of those documents disappeared without a trace. Just as mysteriously, the checks were cashed and the securities redeemed, with all of the money "lost."

The FBI got wind of this situation, and because the interstate post was involved, they started to investigate. Suspicion almost immediately centered on Henry. The FBI discovered that Henry's bank account was growing larger rapidly, and had reached nearly a million dollars. Then suddenly it dropped to near zero.

The FBI's lead investigator decided it was time to pick up Henry for questioning. They waited for him to return from a nearby stamp show and then took him in for questioning. Of course, he had little to say and they had no evidence to hold him, so they let him go.

That evening, Henry went to his favorite restaurant and was seen alone at the bar writing letters and writing in his diary. On the way out, he dropped a slip of paper that proved to be his downfall. The paper was a stub from one of the missing checks.

He was arrested the next day and ultimately convicted of the crime, but the FBI never did locate all of the money he had so recently in his possession. The letters he had been writing the night before had apparently been mailed, but the dairy was taken by the FBI and kept in a secret repository for years as evidence. I found it in a file box marked TOP SECRET while I was applying for a job there, and decided that it should by all rights be housed on Vashon. I took it with the idea of giving it to the Historical Society. The treasure itself is still out there.

The Crystal Cavern

Few people, especially geologists, would think that there was a "snowball's chance" of finding crystals on Vashon or Maury Islands, but I for one can testify to the fact that there are crystals here, and that they do have special powers.

This so-called story I've heard from both long-time islanders and more recent emigrants, some of whom have intimate knowledge of the power of crystals and the magic of each of the minerals. I have no doubt that it is true, at least more or less.

This cavern near Robinwood Beach has inspired numerous raucous celebrations and clandestine meetings, but only a few treasures have been revealed there.

In the mid-to late 19th century, there was an early settler on the island named Georg Hafemittag. Now you'd think with a German name like that, he'd be a bit out of his element in the "PNW," but quite the contrary. Georg was a long-time trapper and fur trader from Canada who eventually went into fishing and logging to make ends meet. He lived on the west side near what is now called Robinwood Beach. After a lot of searching, he eventually found a wife (Lisle, in the fish-mongering community along the Duwamish) and moved her to Vashon, along with her mother and her mother's collection of vintage cigar boxes, to make a comfy home on the heights to the west of the present-day King County dump and landfill. The exact location is lost to time, but legend has it that they lived on a knife-edged ridge above a rushing stream with their house exactly centered between four large cedars.

One day, Georg was out walking the woods (unbeknownst to his wife and her mother) looking for a place to stash some cigar boxes when he stepped over a Sword Fern and dropped into a deep hole, which was really a subterranean cavern. He lit a match in the darkness and discovered that he was surrounded by brilliant crystals, all radiating from the walls of the cavern and pointing directly at him. Taking this as a sign from above and realizing that the crystals had special powers, he gathered a number of them and stuffed them in his rucksack.

On the floor of the cavern was a small stream. This stream appeared to disappear into the wall of the cavern, and Georg assumed that the stream was actually the source of water that he had seen seeping from the hillside farther down on the old Robinwood Road. There were lots of seeps on Robinwood (and to the north closer to Sunset Beach), and this suggested to Georg that there was more than one crystal cavern hidden in the hillside.

Crystals found at various locations on the west side, usually near Robinwood Beach and to the west of the landfill. All of these finds have been isolated surface discoveries. None has led to the location of a larger deposit.

Georg gathered a good number of crystals, and just as his rucksack was getting full, he felt a small tremor. And then another, this time stronger. The cavern shook and a few crystals broke off and fell down. Another tremor broke more crystals, and Georg realized that he'd better get out of there if he ever wanted to see his Lisle again.

Georg looked up to see that the crack he had fallen in was getting smaller, so he scurried up the crystal wall, grabbing onto huge projections and erect crystals in order to get a footing, and eventually flopped out onto the ground next to the crevasse, just as it closed tight. The rumbling stopped and all was quiet.

He was exhausted but he had his sack of powerful crystals, which he thought he could sell for a handsome profit. Lisle had a different idea. She grabbed up the crystals and put them in a pale green Mason jar, screwing on a lid. She told Georg that it was for the benefit of the entire family (presumably meaning her and Georg, as they did not have any children) and that she was saving these for the future, to be kept in a place that only she knew.

One west-side resident dug this shaft looking for a crystal-lined cavern he believed was on his land. This view is looking straight down. I do not usually recommend this type of exploration except in certain cases.

Lisle died tragically in a logging accident just a few months later. A large hemlock log rolled off of a pile of cut timber and squashed her nearly flat. This happened before she had a chance to reveal to Georg the whereabouts of her hiding place.

Georg was never sure just where she put the magical crystals, but when he was close to death he told a close friend that he thought they must be near the old Robinwood Road just as it comes down to the beach. He told the same friend that other clues to its location existed, namely a map that Lisle had sketched, a letter that she had left in their lockbox addressed to her mother, a branch from a tree that grew just above the hiding place, and a four-leaf clover. He did not understand the significance of the clover, but I have an idea about that.

The sketched map surfaced in later years and several people have copies, but it has not yet led to the discovery of the crystals. The tree branch was recovered in an estate sale when Georg died and it proved to be a typical Western Red Cedar branch with no unusual markings. The mysterious letter to the mother is still thought to be missing.

It appears that of all the people who have been looking over the years, only I know where the letter can be found.

The Heron's Nest Bathroom Cold Spot

Few Vashon ghost stories are as well documented as the Heron's Nest Cold Spot. Many islanders have experienced it, and even the business people who work daily in that building freely acknowledge the chilling effect it has had on them and their patrons.

The Heron's Nest is the arts and crafts retail outlet for Vashon Allied Arts, and it is housed in the old commercial building on the southeast corner of Vashon Highway and Bank Road. The cold spot is named after the Heron's Nest in this compilation simply because the arts store is widely known. But the cold spot predates the establishment of the Heron's Nest by several decades at least. No connection is implied with Vashon Allied Arts or the other businesses in that block.

According to at least one elderly island resident, the cold spot was first noticed many decades ago during a particularly cold winter, which makes it even more amazing and mysterious. Fred Spritzer, a local car salesman and aspiring photographer, was looking to use a restroom and found the ones behind the Heron's Nest, at the end of the back hallway. While dropping his drawers, he was immediately struck with a cold chill that seemed to emanate from the room itself. That, coupled with the dim light in the bathroom and some odd noises from the adjoining storage room, convinced him that he was dealing with something supernatural, a haunting unique even for Vashon.

Spritzer shared his thoughts with some of his friends at a nearby tavern, and they returned later that night with Fred's camera to see if they could photograph the hoary specter itself. Indeed, after waiting quietly in a dark corner for several hours, with camera aimed and focused, they did capture an image of a haunted spirit entering the room in a ghostly fashion, floating across the concrete floor noiselessly.

In the turmoil following the flash from the camera, the spirit vanished. But the coldness remained, a testimonial to the longevity of the haunting. And that coldness persists today, evident to everyone who uses those bathrooms or even ventures back into the storage area. The ghost is even known to lock the entrance to the bathrooms, trapping people inside. Clearly, the Heron's Nest bathrooms are a focus of spiritual activity, and a gathering spot perhaps for other disembodied spirits from around the island.

Spritzer's photo went on to be published in a local newspaper. The controversy surrounding its meaning was so intense that one Community Council member was forced to resign and his wife later divorced him. I conclude that this episode is a good example of just how intense is the feeling on Vashon about ghosts. Shortly after, Spritzer left the island in a huff and vowed never to return. He died penniless and unhappy in Enumclaw about 10 years later, having never sold another photograph.

Is the spirit a spurned artist? Or perhaps someone who was unlucky in love? Maybe a logger who was killed in an accident, or a child lost in the surf? Perhaps some enterprising investigator will try again to contact the spirit, and ask him (or her) directly. It's too late to tell Fred, but then again, maybe it's not.

Some of the tools of a treasure hunter, but none of these will help you locate a ghost or exorcise a poltergeist. For those tasks, you'll need special help. If you've seen a ghost on Vashon, contact me.

The Portage Poltergeists, and Other Assorted Hauntings

The Portage Poltergeists have been known for a very long time, so long in fact that like many other ghost stories, people contend that the spirits are Native American in origin. Certainly, this would seem to make sense in this case because both the S'Homamish and the Nisqually peoples used this area extensively in what modern archaeologists call a "resource sharing" arrangement.

For their part, the S'Homamish used the nearby Madrone groves to bury their dead in canoes. This practice led some modern-day Islanders to suggest that the poltergeists are still wandering the Earth because they are perpetually seasick. It also is thought to have inspired "Machine Gun" Morgan to hide his getaway bicycle in a tree.

While the S'Homamish were busy using the trees to lodge their past members, the Nisqually people were putting up bird nets to snag their flying dinners. I postulate that the S'Homamish liked the bird nets because it cut down on the number of birds that would poop on their canoes, which could be the real reason for the establishment of this symbiotic relationship between the two peoples. *[Author's note: In future years, both Maury Island residents and Vashon residents, in a "resource sharing" arrangement, would jointly pay to put up bright reflectors to scare birds away from the overhead power lines. One might conclude that they had grown tired of small birds as a food source. Coincidently, the number of deceased island residents currently left in the trees near Portage has declined to about three per year.]*

The Nisqually people used the Portage area on Tuesdays, Thursdays, and alternate Fridays. The S'Homamish had Mondays, Wednesdays and the remaining Fridays. Saturdays and Sundays were "open use" days, with every Saturday night reserved for private parties (war and Sun dance), weddings, and the like. This arrangement was remarkable for its time, but years and years of such use resulted not only in a dramatic decline of the bird population but a concurrent proliferation of human remains and decrepit canoes. I postulate that it also resulted in one of the largest concentrations of documented poltergeists in the New World.

For instance, there are known to be thirteen homes in the Portage and Kingsbury Beach areas that have resident poltergeists. In one home, an antique player piano belts out tunes by itself, mostly one Bach fugue. In another home, garbage mysteriously appears under the children's beds. In a third, cans of beer disappear without a trace as if sucked into a cosmic abyss. In a home on Raab's Lagoon, the poltergeist rearranges furniture in the living room every night, sometimes waking up the inhabitants by dragging chairs across the floor or running around the dining room table. And in a home fronting Quartermaster Harbor, residents report that they often discover their kayak to be floating out in the harbor, paddling itself around in circles, only to return to shore with the next tide. Clearly, it is no coincidence that the name Kingsbury contains the word "bury."

Perhaps the most dramatic and public manifestation of the Portage poltergeists is at the collection of old exercise bicycles set up along the road. Late on many warm summer nights, these bicycles can be observed exercising on their own, with wheels and pedals turning furiously as if the spirits were working out at a health club. I find that this aspect of the haunting is encouraging. It suggests to me that even disembodied spirits have concern for their general health.

Given the increasing costs of health care, more attention to personal health, regardless of life status, is always a positive development.

This picture taken in about 1956 clearly documents a poltergeist just as it has dislodged this boy's hat. The poltergeist is just outside the frame of the photo, but would not have been visible on Kodachrome film in any case. Ektachrome is the recommended film to capture ghosts in daylight. Digital cameras are of no use whatsoever. For flash pictures in dark settings, use Plus-X.

As you might suspect given the number of old buildings on the islands, there are plenty of other hauntings not described in detail in this compilation. For example, I have reports of a ghost being sighted on the Passenger Only boat (usually on the last trip of the day) that appears to be a haggard businessman with shoddy clothes. Perhaps he committed "career suicide" by losing his temper at a meeting with a stubborn client.

There is also a resident ghost on the ferry Issaquah, but in this case it's a woman in a tie-dyed dress with long flowing hair and no shoes. She is often seen late in the evening near the snack bar, especially if the lights are dimmed. Sometimes she is seen trying to jimmy open the *Beachcomber* rack to get a free paper.

More than one ghost has been sighted at Pt. Robinson, as you might expect, and they are the usual lot of either seaweed-draped sailors covered with bottom-dwelling organisms or ships' engineers who were dismembered in steam explosions. A pfennig a dozen, these kinds of hauntings are.

There used to be a ghost in the building that now houses the Hardware Store Restaurant, but that spirit has apparently moved his venue to the Monkey Tree, where he has been observed drooling over the vegetarian entrees. I surmise he is not a fan of "great good" hunks of meat.

Those of you who have seen real ghosts on Vashon or Maury Islands should send your sighting stories to me at the email address near the front of this book. I will include your story in a subsequent edition if it can be verified, and give you credit besides. However, there are no royalties involved. One cannot make money at the expense of the spirit world and get away with it for long. I know this from personal experience.

This poor man was impoverished after attempting to benefit from offering bogus investment advice to disembodied spirits. Let this be a lesson to you: NEVER *attempt to defraud the dead!*

The South-End Giant Octopus

The south-end giant octopus is not at all a mythical beast. It is well known that the species of octopus that inhabits the waters around Vashon grows rather large. On the south end in particular there are some ledges and "reefs" that provide excellent shelter for this solitary and shy creature. For that reason, there have been many expeditions to seek out this elusive animal, and some of those expeditions have been documented in film on King5's *NW Backroads* and programs on the *Discovery Channel*. One could say that the Vashon giant octopus is a TV star.

What these shows have missed is that there is more to this than just a larger-than-average bit of calamari. If you read the early accounts of exploration in the Puget Sound, and consult the most obscure Native American tales, you'll find a dark and sinister history of sightings and lost boats suggestive of the presence of more than one VERY large octopus. And by VERY large I mean on the order of 120 feet from arm tip to arm tip!

Logs from both the Vancouver and Wilkes voyages contain references to sightings of tentacles measuring several tens of feet in length that momentarily snagged small boats or wrapped around anchor chains. In most cases, the sailors pounded on the tentacles with oars or other tools and the octopus withdrew.

But Vancouver also recounts a tale of one such sailor in a dinghy who was not so lucky. Just as his small boat was approaching Vancouver's mother ship, two tentacles rose from the inky blackness below and wrapped themselves about the dinghy and the poor sailor's arm. Both boat and man were pulled under the waves, everyone being helpless to stop the powerful creature. The dinghy was recovered several days later, missing several boards and much of its hardware. The sailor was never found, but one of his shoes surfaced near the dinghy containing the remains of a foot. Sadly, the sailor's coffin contained only this foot, a fact that Vancouver was careful to keep from the next of kin.

There are other tales of missing boats and drowned swimmers that are almost too numerous to mention. But by far the most exciting is the one that describes my own experience with the evil creature.

In the summer of 1987, I was visiting the Puget Sound area on one of my early trips to the region, having been invited to the area by a young woman I met in the Long Branch Saloon in Livingston, Montana. The motto of the Long Branch is "*Please do not stand while room is in motion*," presumably because they have earthquakes there as well. But it wasn't an earthquake that convinced me that night to travel the entire distance to Vashon in her pickup truck sitting next to her overly active dog, whose name I have forgotten.

Arriving on Vashon in late August, one is understandably smitten with the climate and the grandeur of the scenery. Looking at those mountains, I was entranced with their beauty and resolved to find a way to stay with this woman, even if only for a short time. That opportunity was soon presented when she told me two nights later of a very scary creature that lived close by her Aunt's beach cabin near the south-end ferry dock. She described in minute detail the giant octopus and recounted its depredations upon Auntie's flock of chickens. The octopus had even gotten her prized cock during a night raid.

I surmised that my friend's Aunt, as well as my friend, would be most impressed if I was able to kill (or at least injure) the beast, and so I resolved to battle it the following evening. Thinking that it would be more likely to fall for my "bait" in the coming darkness, I waited until near sundown to launch my borrowed kayak into the waters of Dalco Passage. I had smeared the remains of a seal carcass all over the kayak, thinking that the awful smell would be impossible for the octopus to ignore. I also discovered that it was just as impossible for my friend's dog to ignore. This was my first mistake of the evening.

The ambitious canine followed me into the water in an attempt to capture some of that alluring aroma for himself. His swimming skills proved more than adequate, and he soon caught up to me about 100 yards offshore. Just as he was about to pull himself up and roll onto the kayak, two long and slimy tentacles shot out of the water and wrapped themselves around the dog. Terrified, I could only watch as the poor pooch was pulled into a watery grave.

But Poochie did not surrender without a fight. Up came one tentacle after another, whipping the water into a frenzy and creating a whirlpool that began to turn my small vessel. One tentacle was bloody, another had a tip missing, and then I saw a bit of dog hair stuck to a third. The wild slashing continued for what must have been no more than a minute, and then there was dead silence. Very…dead…silence.

I recovered my paddle and began working my way back to shore, my kayak smelling of dead seal and having a new leak as a result of being thrashed by the beast. Imagine my surprise when I paddled into shore and there on the beach, soaking wet and wagging his ragged tail, was my friend's trusty canine pal, holding a bit of tentacle in his mouth.

"Poochie," the Octopus Slayer.

Needless to say, the dog's homecoming was celebrated with a bit more enthusiasm than was mine. Unlike me, he wasn't held responsible for the damage to the kayak, nor had he done anything to endanger my girl's best friend. AND he had battled the giant octopus and won! Good dog!

So I left the next day smelling of dead seal and suffering a bruised ego. The dog walked me to the ferry dock, I presume to get one more chance at rolling on that smell.

Unusually friendly deer are often found near sideways-growing Alders (next story), but you must be careful around them because like most animals they communicate using ESP. Dogs, for instance, do this as well and take many of their instructions from a planet that orbits a star in the constellation Ursa Major.

Sideways-Growing Alders

I surmise that when most of you think of trees, you think of them as growing straight up, pointing to the heavens. Certainly, this is the way normal trees grow, but on Vashon and Maury Islands, there are trees that show a different habit, one so rare and disturbing that it can only be caused by some dark force unknown to man. I am referring here to the mysterious sideways-growing Alders.

I have seen sideways-growing Alders mostly around the edges of the islands, such as on Glen Acres Road, Bachelor Road, Hake Road, and low on the west side. There are some very ancient ones on the north side of Maury Island and others above the shoreline both east and west of the north-end ferry terminal.

Unlike normal Red Alders that grow straight up, these grow out to the side, sometimes just 20 degrees or so above the horizontal. Rarely, they will even grow downward. These trees appear similar to the quills on a porcupine, with ones on the top of the hill pointing up, and ones on the sides pointing out or down.

The reason for this unusual growth pattern is a complete mystery. Scientists have studied these trees for years and found nothing about them that is different from upright Alders, but scientists can only measure what they suspect exists. If what you are measuring is outside the capacity of your measuring technique, then clearly you will not collect any meaningful data. For example, you would not try to measure the presence or absence of a ghost using a common yardstick.

It is for the above reason that I decided to test the Alders with my own measurement system. I employed the assistance of two local psychics, who were tied to heavy chairs (for safety, in case they fell asleep) and placed about 200 yards apart in a large grove of sideways Alders just above a west-side beach. The psychics were instructed to tap into the cosmic energy of the trees and probe their auras for answers, acting as concerned humans interested only in the health of the forest.

Despite their objections, the two psychics were left there overnight because it is well known that trees communicate mostly in the darkness when they are not busy with photosynthesis. Unfortunately, a fierce storm came up that night that resulted in the largest March rainfall on record.

Looking straight down the cliff at a cluster of Alders that committed suicide; this example is from Lower Quartermaster Harbor.

At daylight, I went looking for the psychics and found only a large bare patch of mud where one had been, most of the trees in his area now residing on the beach. As to how they got there I have no clue. Perhaps they committed suicide. Tree suicide pacts are widely known from the Mississippi Delta and other locales including Quartermaster Harbor (see photo above). Or perhaps the trees decided to sacrifice themselves for the health of Puget Sound, voluntarily adding a significant amount of "large woody debris" to the critical intertidal zone. It is hard to say what came over them, but I did recover the chair later.

The second psychic was still in his original location, albeit a bit damp and covered with leaves. He reported that indeed he was able to connect during the night with the surrounding trees and sense their distress at the approaching storm, but his communication was cut short after he was knocked cold by a hail stone. He never had a chance to ask why they grew sideways, and according to the Deputy Prosecutor, we won't have a chance to repeat this experiment.

Epilogue

I've been searching for treasures of all sorts for most of my life. From simple fossils as a young child, to artifacts of early man as a teenager, to rare minerals including gold and silver as a young adult, and finally to lost mines and buried treasures of all sorts as a mature man.

I have searched for, and found, precious antiques, lost coins, gold nuggets, valuable artworks, human skeletons, ancient pottery, evidence of alien civilizations, rare stamps, letters and diaries from famous people, and miraculous wonders of nature seen by few men. I have witnessed events unique in the human experience, been places others can only imagine, and stood in places so uncommon that to others it would be like traveling to the Moon.

I have found ancient Incan fortresses in Bolivia, golden samovars in Russia, prehistoric copper axes in Michigan, Viking rune stones in Mexico, the remains of an alien spacecraft in the Pacific Northwest, a valise filled with Confederate money in Missouri, Roman ruins along the eastern seaboard of the United States, and an Egyptian pyramid in the Antarctic.

I have been shot three times, stabbed, bitten by poisonous snakes, struck by lightning, chased by wild dogs, robbed of all my possessions, thrown in filthy prisons, beaten by corrupt soldiers, and written up in newspapers as a complete idiot.

Thieves and bandits have stolen my clothes, automobile,

money, passport, wife (later returned), wedding ring, camera, personal jet, and favorite hat.

Through all of this, I have learned one important lesson: ***If you search for something long enough, no matter what it is, you will surely find it.***

But I also have one warning for you, Intrepid Searcher, something that you must never, in all your searching and all your travels, ever forget: ***When you find it, the treasure for which you've been seeking may not be quite what you expected.***

Checklist for Treasure Hunters

Preparation is the key to successful treasure hunting. You need the right tool for the right job, as my wife and life partner reminds me daily. And so she should!! Just think what would happen, for example, if I stumbled across a mine shaft to explore and had left home that day without any extra flashlight batteries? In years past, I'd have gone to the nearest residence and "scrounged" some batteries, but these days I must rely upon my own resourcefulness, partly because of a misguided judgment from the Superior Court of Arizona.

For the benefit of the novice, I have compiled a list of some of the essential items every treasure hunter should have at his or her disposal. All of these items should be arranged in a backpack or carrying case that is handy for the field. You never know when the exploring "bug" is going to bite, so keep your treasure hunting "kit" near the door. Once a week, check the freshness of the items that might spoil, such as the food rations and batteries.

I believe that all of the items listed are essential to your success, but you may find that you can substitute some items for others to fit your individual needs, and I may have forgotten a few things. Even so, always take care to include tools sufficient to insure success in the area you are working. For example, you may not need a box of matches if you are working near an active volcano, but if you leave them out when you go trekking in the Alaskan wilderness in January, rescuers may find you later in the form of a giant Popsicle.

Important Notes:

Never EVER let another person use your kit, because even a seemingly harmless oversight by another can put your life in danger. Once, for example, I allowed a friend to borrow my kit, and he used my climbing rope to wipe some peanut butter off of his pocket knife. Later, I was using that rope to rappel down the face of Half Dome in Yosemite National Park, and it snapped. Few people are aware that peanut butter is extremely corrosive and is used to etch glass and clean metal for welding operations. Because of my friend's ignorance, I had to spend six weeks in hospital and pay for a new roof for the senior park ranger's cabin.

Lastly, the list below is suitable for ***day trips only***. For overnight trips, add such extra items as you might need to go camping, such as a bed roll and/or tent.

The items you will need in your treasure hunting kit:

- **Food** – Take enough for three days even though you plan to be gone one. A can of sardines and a tomato can last me for three days in a pinch. Or you can learn which plants and mushrooms are edible. It is best to do this beforehand rather than through trial and error.
- **Canteen and water purification tablets** – Take at least a gallon of water with you (in cool weather) for each day you plan to be out, more if it's hot. When you run out, look for water in roadside puddles, old stumps, and flowing streams. After a few years of drinking contaminated water, you'll be used to most pathogens, but use purification tablets in the meantime. Springs can be hints to

hidden caverns. If you are headed into the desert, carry lots more water. Some people take ten gallons at least.

- **First aid kit** – Normally, I think first aid kits are for Tenderfoot Boy Scouts and other inexperienced explorers, but it is proper (and a matter of liability avoidance) to say you should have one with you. Once you've been around the block like I have, you'll know how to make a splint from anything at hand, such as an inner tube or case of canned beans.
- **Sunscreen or a good hat** – I hiked for years without either, but now I visit the dermatologist twice a year.
- **Rain poncho** – Unless you're Mary Poppins, a poncho is better than an umbrella. You can't fold up an umbrella.
- **Extra socks and underwear** – The need for extra underwear should be obvious. With respect to socks, just remember that success on any front is all about proper foot care.
- **A good map of the area** – You need to know where you are at all times, and to stay away from private property unless you have permission from the owner. I learned this the hard way.
- **Map case** – Keep your map and your matches dry at all times.
- **Matches** – I think everyone should be required to know how to make a fire with just two sticks, but since the advent of the Iron Age, we've had flint and steel, which is a lot easier. I once won a fire-starting competition using flint and steel. Honest.
- **Ball of string** – This is not for finding your way home but for making tools and animal traps, just in case. It is

also widely known that cougars will chase a thrown ball of string.

- **Waterproof notebook** – Important to any serious treasure hunter is the practice of taking thorough notes. "Write! Write! Write!" said my 7th grade grammar teacher, and she was certainly correct. All great explorers and reputable archaeologists take copious notes and write extensive journals. Just look at Indiana Jones in all of his movies…he did nothing but write from the beginning until the end, didn't he?
- **Pencils, plain and colored** – For writing notes and making sketch maps in your waterproof notebook. Or you could use your knife to create a convenient blood pen by poking a hole in your fingertip (these pens are always "at hand"). If you do this, keep the snake bite remedy nearby for use as an antiseptic.
- **Compass** – For finding your way to the treasure and for finding your way home. Also, in the presence of magnetic masses, the compass will spin, so use yours to find buried alien spacecraft and iron meteorites.
- **Climbing rope and hardware** – At least 100 feet with all the accompanying climbing hardware. And you'd better take a rock climbing class first unless you want to be scraped off the rocks with a spatula.
- **Geiger counter or scintillometer** – Helpful when trying to locate materials that had their origin either in outer space or at Hanford Nuclear Reservation.
- **Portable UV light** – This is for locating fluorescent materials and scorpions in the dark, and for doing scary stuff at Halloween. Don't look directly at one; it's bad for your eyes.

- **Hammer and chisel** – For hammering and chiseling things.
- **Machete or Bowie knife** – Forget the pistol, a machete is ever so much more intimidating. But really, it's just for whacking at blackberries. Be careful when you use one, or you may be giving your field partner a new nickname, such as "Lefty."
- **Camera** – For taking pictures of what you've found, because photographic proof is much more convincing than just your word, and you're going to need all the proof you can get.
- **Extra film or memory card** – You can't take too many pix.
- **Mineral testing kit** – This is for mature audiences only, because if you put together a good mineral test kit, you'll need toxic chemicals like Borax, Sodium Carbonate, and dilute Hydrochloric Acid. Check out Dana's *Manual of Mineralogy* for more information.
- **Mirror for signaling** – A bit dated, perhaps, but in the back country the Sun never goes out of style. You can also use it for shaving (with a really sharp machete, or a dull one if you don't require a clean shave) if you're out for a while.
- **Surveying instruments** – In case you need to make a map or need to document the exact location of something important, like a disputed property line or an off-limits bombing range. You should be aware of those things.
- **Carbide mine lamp and extra carbide** – Forget flashlights that constantly need batteries. Carbide lamps are classic, fun, and great for impressing others. In 30 years

of using them, I've only had one blow up on me (honestly) so their hazardous nature is somewhat exaggerated. It is not true that the Great Chicago Fire started with a malfunctioning carbide lamp, however some conspiracy theorists note that fragments were found in the remains of the second WTC tower collapse.

- **Gold pan** – Just a small one, because you won't be carrying a large shovel to support using a larger one. Clearly, this is for testing gravel and sand for the presence of gold and other heavy minerals, but I've also used a gold pan to fry chicken (really) and prepare whole meals while camping. Some are already lined with Teflon, so why not? Don't get a plastic one, because they don't do so well in the fire.
- **Small folding shovel or entrenching tool** – For digging dirt, mostly, when searching for treasures, but it's also handy for digging field latrines and covering up "evidence" of your presence. Don't forget a roll of TP. Big leaves work, too, but unless you know the difference between Oregon Grape and Poison Oak, you may be taking a chance with your keister.
- **Snake bite remedy** – Last but not least, you need about a quart of proven snake bite remedy, at least 80 proof. Any brand will do. It has many uses in the field, notably as an antiseptic, stimulant, coolant, and fire starter. Snakes don't like it either.

Field Notes (Write! Write! Write!)

Field Notes (Write! Write! Write!)

Field Notes (Write! Write! Write!)

Field Notes (Write! Write! Write!)

CPSIA information can be obtained
at www.ICGtesting.com
Printed in the USA
FSHW011258130821
84062FS

9 781432 762995